I0531096

Breathe With Me
Dahlia Schweitzer

THE BAO HOUSE
TORONTO * LOS ANGELES * NEW YORK CITY

Breathe With Me
Dahlia Schweitzer

Copyright © 2013 Dahlia Schweitzer

Also available from Dahlia Schweitzer:

Lovergirl
Seduce Me
I've Been a Naughty Girl
Queen of Hearts
Another Kind of Monster: Cindy Sherman's Office Killer

This book is dedicated to Alastair and StoryWonk, without whom my words would merely lie flat on the page. Thank you for bringing them to multi-dimensional life!

Sunday night

There was never a good night to run into an ex, but a Sunday night in Los Angeles was worse than most. The bars were vacant, the drinking more desperate, the knowledge of Monday looming over everything. I had not wanted to go out, but I did not want to stay home, either. Ever since becoming single again, Sundays had that restless feeling I remembered them having in high school, the nervousness of what the next week would bring ruining the last moments of the weekend.

Television was never enough of a distraction, and so here I was, pulling into a half-empty parking lot belonging to one of those east L.A. bars that never really fill up during the week but certainly do not stand a chance on a Sunday. I was more punctual than usual, ready to meet my friends and kill some time until I could fall asleep. Just another wasted weekend.

I felt the anxious desperation of the single made visual in the makeup I had applied in my too bright bathroom, fueled by a desire to forget I would be going home alone. There was a fine line between artfully applied lip gloss and looking like a drag queen, and I never felt like I balanced it well. Just a little too much of the sparkly pink eye shadow, and I looked like Amanda Lepore's stand-in. At least it was dark in here, and I savored my immunity from the cruel exposure of fluorescent bulbs. Perhaps the dim lighting would soften the rough touches of my awkward application.

I leaned against the bar, scanning the room while making half-hearted conversation with my friends, all of whom exuded the easy poise of the attached or married. It felt grim, the only potential highlight the bartender with her tight jeans and shiny hair. I hated crowded bars, but at least then there was a larger market from which to choose.

1

You can't have everything, I thought, sighing, trying not to be too eager to get back home.

The first drink was innocent. The second intentional. The third an undecided possibility as I got up to go to the bathroom. I was losing the battle between being "positive" and going home to get in bed with my laptop and some CSI episodes. Technically, one could say I slept with William Petersen.

I decided to go to the bathroom to check my makeup, to confirm whether I was still making Amanda proud, and to collect my not-quite-sober thoughts, in a last ditch effort to focus and make this evening salvageable. If I managed just one phone number, I could go home happy. One serious stare in the bathroom mirror, accompanied by an equally serious personal talking-to, could be all that stood between me and accomplishment.

Leaving my friends at the bar, I was all business, in pursuit of that all-elusive positive attitude, and that's when I saw him. He was just pulling his I.D. out of his wallet. He had not seen me yet, but I knew it was him immediately.

When you spend a year with someone, you know who they are without seeing their face. You have their posture, the way they move, and the way they breathe, etched into your brain. Even in the shadow of the doorway, even under his hat, I knew it was him, and I froze. I did not know what to do. Should I run? What a ridiculous idea. Run where? Into the bathroom? The bar was so small; he would see me as soon as I came out.

So I decided not to postpone the inevitable. I just stood there, waiting for him to put his wallet back in his pocket and discover me. I swallowed at the glimpse of his hips before averting my eyes to the safe neutrality of the bar. It still hurt that I saw him and could not touch him. I missed running my hand along his hips—and everything else.

I exhaled slowly. I tried to remember yogic breathing. I waited for him to look at me.

He noticed me a few seconds later. I smiled. He smiled

2

back, stepping into the bar.

"Hey, Max," I said.

"Hey, Lori," he said.

I reached forward to put my arms around him. I felt him close, an instant of intimacy in the guise of formality. I smelled him, his mixture of deodorant and aftershave. For a moment, I thought nothing would stop me from going home with him, from falling asleep to that smell and the feel of his body, but then I remembered that we were not doing that anymore, and so I let go.

"Nice to see you," I said.

"Nice to see you," he said.

We stared at each other. Were we standing a little too close for exes who were not allowed to sleep with each other? If I stepped back further, would that be rude? If I stepped forward, would he push me away? Was he looking at me with more intensity than he should? Were his lips closer than society allowed?

I could not read his body language. Had I wanted him this much when we were together? My mind raced with questions, all of them fundamentally irrelevant. Nothing was going to happen, and I knew it. The breakup had been dramatic and final.

"How are things?" he asked.

"Things are good."

He was wearing a green hat that I had never seen before. It must be new. There must have been a lot of new things that he had gotten since I had seen him last. Had he also gotten a new girlfriend?

"Are you seeing someone?" I wanted to ask, but I could not. I did not want him to know that I wanted to know, and I did not know what I would do with the answer. If he said no, would I be disappointed that he was single and still not interested in me? If he said yes, would I feel shattered because I wanted him for myself? And how would he interpret the fact that I cared enough to ask in the first place?

So I decided to stick with safety.

3

"How are things?" I asked.

"Good," he replied, nodding, doing that noncommittal guy shrug thing.

His jacket was buttoned up to his collarbone even though it was another warm L.A. night. I wondered what he was wearing underneath. I thought about what would be underneath that. I could remember so clearly the way he looked in my mind that it seemed unfair no amount of recollection could make the memories real again. He had this soft skin, lightly covered with blonde hair, but now a jacket stood between that chest and me. It was a darker green than the hat, vaguely military in cut, and it looked amazing on him.

Of course, in my current state, I would probably have been seduced by an ordinary t-shirt or a bulky leather jacket (two favorites of his when we had been together) but this outfit, after those two drinks and half a year of unrequited desire, seemed like the epitome of style and seduction.

Until my friends appeared out of nowhere.

"What's going on, Lori?" Rachel asked.

"Yeah, where'd you go?" Laura asked.

"Did you want that drink?" Sara asked.

They all stared at him. They knew who he was—and why he was persona non grata. I knew they were right, and I knew I should turn away with just a polite nod, but I still wished they would be the ones to disappear into holes in the floor, leaving me alone with him again, so I could recapture whatever pretense of a moment I had been pretending we were having.

They were my friends, though, which meant they were not going to let me even *entertain* the notion of hooking up with my ex. We all just stood there, one grand party in the foyer of a crappy bar, conversation flowing with no real direction while I tried to laugh but contributed nothing. He stared silently, until it got too awkward, and then he said he had to go, leaving us for the bar. I tried to ignore the disappointment in my gut.

4

"What was that about?" Sara asked.

"Nothing. Nothing."

"You okay?" Rachel looked at me with concern.

"Yeah, yeah, I'm fine." I glanced over. He was sitting at the bar, talking to some guy with a hooded sweatshirt. If he had been meeting a girl, I would have died.

"Come back to the table. The hot bartender's been asking about you," said Laura, smiling.

"For real?"

"Yeah." She nodded, with an even bigger grin. "And I don't think it's because of your tips. She wanted to know if you kiss girls, if you know what I mean…"

"And what did you tell her?"

"What do you think I told her? I told her only the hot ones!" She laughed.

I looked at the bartender. Laura was right. On a scale of hot bartenders, this lady was at least a ten, if not off the scale entirely. It was not so much the hair (short brown layers framing her face, brushing across her shoulders), or her eyes (greenish hazel brown), or the leanly defined arms (Pilates?), but the way they all slid together—the easy angular stance, the cool confidence, the lips sticky with clear lip-gloss. Even gum was sexy in her mouth.

She dropped some bills into the change glass and tilted her head up. We made eye contact. She winked. All my friends saw it.

"See?!" Rachel exclaimed, shoving me in a manner more typical to junior high cafeteria romantic trysts than grown-up bars.

"You know you want it…" Laura whispered loudly—and drunkenly—in my ear.

"Come on. Let's get that third drink," Sara said, grabbing hold of my sleeve and tugging me toward our seats.

I glanced toward the other bar. My ex was still talking to Mr. Hooded Sweatshirt. I looked back at Ms. Hot Bartender. She was making a drink for some guy with a knit cap.

5

"Come *on*," tugged Sara.

What do you do?

The ex? *(turn to page 7)*
or
The hottie bartender? *(turn to page 12)*

The ex

I knew I should not, but I could not resist. It had been half a year since we had been in the same room, and yet here I was, and here *he* was, apparently alone. I had to take advantage of the situation.

"Sorry, girls," I said. "Give me a couple minutes for this one, and then I'll come join you."

They looked at each other. I knew what they were thinking, but I did not care.

"I need to do this. I'll be back in a few."

This was my life, and it was up to me to make my own mistakes. Leaving before they had a chance to figure out what to say, I made my way over to his end of the bar.

"Is this seat free?" I asked, gesturing to the stool beside him.

He looked at me, looked at the stool, and smiled, nodding.

I scooted onto the seat, feeling like a twenty-one year old on her first date to her first bar. The stool felt extra tall, my legs extra short, and the sweat on my palms disconcerting. I grinned at him nervously. His blue eyes looked back at me.

"It's nice to see you," he said. "How are things?"

I could not help laughing.

"What?"

"We've had this conversation. A few minutes ago. Why don't you buy me a drink, and we'll start a new one?"

He laughed. "Good idea."

Turning to the bartender closest to us (not as attractive as my lady), he took care of my margarita and his whiskey. Then he turned back to me, sliding my drink over.

"Cheers," he said, lifting up his glass.

"Cheers," I said, lifting up mine.

7

We could not stop staring at each other. I wondered when would be the right moment to kiss him and if that moment would ever come.

"How's school?" he asked me. "How's life treating you?"

The ubiquitous questions. I smiled, not even fully conscious of what I was saying. I stammered something about my classes, about having picked my summer schedule, about the final papers I had recently turned in, about the really great independent project I was working on, even giving him a rushed summary of a photo essay I had just completed. Part of me wanted to share these mundane details, wanted to feel that rush of including him in my life again, while another part of me kept racing ahead to edit out any bits that might bore him, the extraneous elements that might make him lose interest, turn around in his seat, and offer a drink to someone else.

Of course, I also wanted to find an offhand manner in which to ask him, "So, are you seeing anyone?" But I still could not ask, because there was no answer I knew how to process. Better not to know and let his actions tell me what he wanted.

So I asked him about his life, and, while he told me about recent drama at his job, I tried to look entertained, appreciating the openness which had been denied me for so long, while also using the opportunity to slide my stool a couple inches closer, reclining on my left hand, as my right hand shifted toward his thigh. He did not notice.

He did, however, notice when I unbuttoned my shirt, revealing the tight tank top I had on underneath. Luckily, I had worn a push-up bra that evening, and, out of the corner of my eye, I could see the excellent view of my freshly exposed cleavage. I knew he could also see it, even though he was subtle, because there was a pause in his anecdote, and a blink, before he continued. I smiled. This was progress.

I let him keep talking, but I had stopped listening. Instead, I kept making sure my breasts were nicely

8

displayed. I slid further over so that I was even closer, so that our faces were not quite so far apart. The kissing moment I was hoping for did not come easily. It rarely does the first time. It was preceded, instead, by the slow procession of knee to knee, shoulders brushing, hands glancing thighs—until, eventually, the inevitable.

No, not the kiss. Time to leave.

Max stood up first. I was in no position to be initiating a separation. If it was up to me, I would have made this night last another fourteen hours.

"I really should be going," he said, standing in front of me with an expression I could not decipher.

I stood up, too. What else could I do?

"I'll walk you out," I said.

"Don't you want to say goodbye to your friends?" he asked, nodding at the other end of the room. I had totally forgotten about them, but they were still there, busy drinking drinks supplied by the hottie bartender.

I smiled. "I'll come back and say goodbye to them after I say goodbye to you."

I did not want to risk screwing up this departure with possible complications, or peanut gallery comments, from my friends. As much as I loved them, I did not trust them to let me make my own bad judgments. And there was a lot riding on this moment.

Grabbing my coat, I followed him out to the parking lot. He leaned against his car, looking at me.

"It's been great to see you again," he said.

I was not going to open my mouth and say something potentially messy, so I just leaned over and hugged him. Despite all the teasing physicalities from our brief time at the bar, this felt like our first real physical contact. I breathed him in, the warm pressure of his arms against me. It reminded me of all the countless embraces we had shared, but this one was different. It had a funny combination of intimacy and foreignness—as though we had just met while, at the same time, it also felt like we had known each other

9

forever. I pressed myself against him. I did not want to let go.

He was not rushing to let go, either. I felt the pressure of his desire between my legs, and my face flushed with excitement. I pressed harder, wrapping my arms tighter. He still had the power to make my skin tingle without doing anything.

Our heads were so close that it only took the slightest movement to tilt back, and then our lips were touching. He did not back away, his hips solidly against mine. I felt the soft wetness of his lips. If he had not been gripping me so tightly, I might have done a romantic swoon. I kissed him, full on. A proper movie-magic kiss that sent shivers down my spine and made him give out the smallest of moans. Oh, how I craved him.

My hands slid around his hips and into the pockets of his pants. I slipped my fingers inside, feeling his skin that much closer, the denim fabric out of the way, only the thin fabric sleeve of the pocket between me and the thighs I desired. I had always loved his thighs, strong and meaty and soft, so real and so masculine, and I gripped him with my fingers, making him moan.

I pushed my right hand deeper into his pocket, further along the inside of his thigh, toward that area I still fantasized about when I masturbated. If I pushed just enough, my fingers reached his beautiful cock, and if I had not felt it, I still would have known that I had reached it, because he collapsed just a bit. I could feel his moan in my mouth, his kisses strengthening in their intensity, his tongue shoved so far inside me that I almost could not breathe.

I reached further, feeling even more of him against my fingers, and I stayed there, fingers stretching the limits of fabric, while his tongue rammed down my throat. I pushed myself against him as much as I could. It was as perfect as you could get it in a parking lot in Los Angeles on a Sunday night, before he gently disentangled, looking down at me with a smile on his face, the weakness of sexual frustration

10

in his eyes.

"I think that's as far as we should go tonight," he said, his tone heavy with the struggle of self-restraint.

"Are you sure?" I asked, trying to sound more playful than desperate.

"Not a hundred percent, but enough to go on." Max laughed, leaning over and kissing me on cheek. "I'll see you."

With one last hug—significantly shorter and less interesting—he got in his car and drove away.

I wanted to stamp my foot. I wanted to shout with sexual frustration and annoyance. How could he do this? What a tease. What a fuck. What a manipulative ass.

I wanted him, and I wanted him *now*. And I knew he wanted me. So why did he do this? Why did he leave like that? I felt the wetness dripping all over my underwear, surely staining my pants by this point, as I looked over at my car and wondered what to do.

What do you do?

Get in the car and drive home to your vibrator?
(turn to page 27)
or
Go back to the bar to seduce the hottie bartender?
(turn to page 34)
or
Go meet your ex at his house?
(turn to page 36)

The hottie bartender

It was time to let bygones be bygones. My friends were right. I had done everything I could to get him back, nothing had worked, and now it was time for someone else's pretty face. Even if I had gone further with my ex, all I would have gotten were some hot and heavy kisses in the parking lot, but I knew he would regret it in the morning, and then I would just feel worse.

Hottie bartender it would be. I smiled first at my friends, who knew exactly what was going on, and then I smiled at her. She winked at me, coming over to wipe down our side of the counter.

"What can I get you girls?" she asked, staring straight at me.

"Lori is going to have her third margarita. And a beer for me, scotch and soda for her, and a vodka tonic for her," Sara said, gesturing at each of us in turn.

All the girls sat back down, making sure to shove me to the left, so that I would be seated near the end of the bar, where there was space for the bartenders and barbacks to get in and out. Clearly, they wanted me exposed and available, and I felt okay with that. Knowing that my ex was twenty feet away made me even more determined to get this girl to touch me. Six months of chastity had been too long. I had to get over him, and she was here, available, and hot. Totally and completely hot.

I watched her making the drinks. Her jeans fit snugly around her hips, riding just low enough that I could see the tips of her hips, reminding me why I fell for girls over and over. Men never looked like that in jeans.

The curve of her waist, the smoothness of the skin between pants and top. Even if I had not been smarting from the pain of rejection, I would covet the feel of her, aching to have her beneath my fingers, wanting to know the exact shape of her stomach, how far I could reach between her legs without needing to open her pants.

I started to imagine grabbing her right there, getting her when she came back with the drinks, gripping her pants with my hand and yanking her to me, spreading my legs while I sat on the barstool, dragging her body between my legs, wrapping myself around her, and feeling her breath on my face for that split second before I shoved my tongue down her throat...

"Here you go, ladies," she said, spreading our drinks in front of us, looking evenly at each before ending her stare on me.

I smiled back at her, and the world dropped away. She was even better up close. Her bangs fell gently across her forehead, slanted in diagonal lines that made me envision her hair messed up across my pillow. Her eyebrows were fine and delicate, framing a pair of saucy brown eyes that were trained directly into mine. I blushed. I wanted to taste her so desperately that I did not know if I could wait until the bar cleared out.

I did not know what to do first.

"She wants you," whispered Laura into my ear.

"I want *her*," I whispered back, watching her walk back down the length of the bar.

"Ooooooooh!" Laura giggled. "This is going to be awesome."

She turned to Sarah, whispering in her ear.

Sarah laughed and looked at me. "Go get her, champ!"

"Shut *up*!" I exclaimed, mortified. The bartender had to have heard.

Ms. Hottie Bartender glanced over her shoulder from down the bar. I shook my head at her, as if to say no big deal, nothing to see here. She smiled, turning back to her customers. I studied her ass. It was perfect. Tight, compact, round—beautiful. I sighed.

"What are you waiting for?" asked Rachel, leaning

13

across Sarah and Laura so that her face was close to mine.

"What am I supposed to do?" I whispered back. "She's working!"

"Well, find out when she stops!" Rachel looked at me, smiling. "We'll be here for you, babe. We'll stay 'til she finishes."

At least that was something. The next time Ms. Hottie came back to our end, I leaned over the bar, making sure she got a shot of my cleavage down my v-necked top, as I asked her what time she got off.

"One hour," she said, grinning. "There's not much time left." She winked.

I could not quite believe it. She was flirting with me!

The next hour went by in a blur of drinks and music and sexual expectation. Every time she came back down to our end, there was something. A wink. A smile. Soon I got more ballsy and started touching her. First, it was just a quick stroke on the arm. Then it was a reach around the end of the bar to her waist. After much urging on the part of my friends and the completion of yet another drink, I even touched her ass. She grinned and told me I was getting feisty. I laughed.

"I like feisty girls, don't you?" I asked, naughtily. Alcohol was making me brave.

She smiled, bangs whisking across forehead, eyes brown and warm in my direction. "I'm flirting with you, aren't I?"

I smiled, happy to hear her say it. It had not been my imagination. Every time she came down to our end of the bar, my friends cooperated and ignored us. Pretending to be absorbed in conversation, they consistently left me alone to talk with her. As the night grew later, and the crowd grew thinner, she spent more and more time coming in my direction. During the last fifteen minutes of her shift, between rinsing glasses and putting away bottles, she talked to me exclusively.

Her name was Natalie. Everything else, I did not register. Whenever she got close, I became mesmerized by

14

the light dash of freckles across her nose, by the way her lips curved, and by the increasing wetness between my legs at the prospect of getting to touch more than a quick inch of her skin.

Fifteen minutes became fourteen, ten, five, and then none were left. My friends did their best to look whichever way was other while Natalie stood beside me.

"I'm done," she said. "What do you want to do? You want to go dance? Or do you want to go back to my place?"

I had not expected options. I glanced over at my friends, but they were offering no support. They were too busy pretending that they were not listening. I sighed, looking back at Natalie. I was tempted by both options. This girl was guaranteed to be amazing on the dance floor, plus I was still buzzed enough that the dark dance floor beckoned tantalizingly. We had been listening to the DJ the whole time we had been there, even if I had been too distracted to pay him proper attention, and his beats were good. I glanced at the dance floor and then back at her slightly gyrating hips while her fingers tapped the rhythm on the bar.

At the same time, if we stayed to dance, I might lose the offer to head to her place. But was that too much too soon anyway? Maybe I *should* try some dance floor booty first?

What do you do?

The dance floor booty?
(turn to page 16)
or
Her place?
(turn to page 21)

15

Dance floor booty

The night seemed long, and I liked the idea of getting dirty with this foxy lady on the dance floor. Plus, that option also allowed room for indulging the ulterior motive of making my ex jealous. I knew he was still there, twenty feet away, even if I was currently mesmerized by my latest crush.

I grabbed her hand, pulling her toward the DJ and his records. The dance floor was pretty empty by this point, only five people twisting and turning, but that worked just fine for me. I hated feeling cramped when I danced, and I knew that all I wanted was to wrap my arms around her and feel her moving against me. As long as I could close my eyes and do that, nothing else mattered—and if I could avoid getting bumped into in the process, so much the better.

I loved the feeling of her hand, the smooth and soft fingers curved around mine, and I did not want to let it go, but when we got to our desired position in front of the DJ booth, she slipped her hand away. I went to grab her waist, but she shook her head, smiling.

"I want you to watch you," she said.

"But I want to touch you," I said. I was greedy for more.

She looked at me, the pulsing beats a background for our mini-cinematic moment.

"Okay, but just give me a couple minutes of looking at you first."

I agreed, leaning up against the DJ booth, wishing I had a cigarette in my hand, feeling incredibly awkward. It took all of thirty seconds for that moment to pass, for me to forget about my awkwardness, thirty seconds of watching her, two feet in front of me, swaying her hips, lifting her arms over her head, running her hands over her body, down her neck, across her stomach, her eyes never leaving mine. I wanted to

16

touch her so desperately that I could not think of anything else. I became transfixed by the tiny stain of sweat that appeared just under her breasts every time she raised her arms, and I knew that stain of sweat was tracing the line of her bra, and I imagined what it looked like, and what it would look like off.

She was wearing a white wife-beater type tank, and she had cut the end of it so that it grazed the top of her jeans, which meant that I kept seeing flesh every time her arms lifted. I found myself wondering how she would taste between my teeth. I wanted to gnaw on her, to feel her sweet softness against my lips and underneath my tongue. Most of all, I wanted to dance with her, so I got up from my pose against the DJ booth and joined her on the dance floor. At first, I was very aware of my ex, mentally evaluating his angle and ability to watch what was happening, but I soon forgot about him. I closed my eyes and wrapped my arms around her, letting the music fill my head and her body press up against everything else.

There are few things more erotic that you can do with another person (especially when fully clothed) than dancing. The style of music or the style of dancing did not matter. If you were wrapped around each other, it was hot. And what was even hotter? When the sexy bartender you had been eyeing all evening wraps her arms around yours, her breasts pressed against yours, and her fingers lightly slipping between your stomach and the top of your pants. The fact that I was wearing pretty low pants only improved the situation. I knew, when her fingers ran across my front, that she could feel the beginnings of my pubic hair, and I tilted my pelvis toward her, encouraging her to dig deeper.

The dance floor was so dark that I did not think anyone would notice our behavior, and if they did, I did not care. All I cared about was her hand between my legs, and the deeper she got, the more I wanted my hand between her legs, but her pants were too tight for my hand to fit anywhere. I had to content myself with my hands on her ass, on her hips, or on her waist, feeling the small curve of her lower back, all the while doing whatever I could to press her closer to me.

"Want to get another drink?" she shouted in my ear, over the sound of the DJ's current record.

I nodded, and she grabbed my hand, pulling me toward the bar. She kept me close while talking to the bartender. I could not hear what she said until she turned to me and said, her lips right beside my ear, "I got you another margarita, hope that's okay?"

I smiled and nodded again. Distracted by the bartender's movements, I was jolted back to the moment by Natalie's hand sliding its way up my shirt and rapidly, before I even knew what was going on, unhooking my bra. Twisting me to face her, she smiled. With two quick tugs, my bra was in her hand.

She grinned at me, sticking the bra in the back pocket of my jeans.

"It's better without," she said, and I blushed, feeling hyperaware of my nipples jutting through the thin fabric of my top.

With a quick glance over her shoulder to confirm that the drinks had been deposited on the counter and that the bartender had moved on to his next customers, she leaned against the bar and, grabbing my belt loops in her fingers, she pulled me closer, tracing the shape of my nipples.

"So pretty…"

I smiled. I liked her being in charge.

My body was still pressed up against hers while her body was pressed up against the bar. She opened the top button of my pants, giving her just enough leverage to reach inside. I felt her tug on my g-string, and I tilted my hips to make it easier for her to reach between my legs. With my eyes closed, my body leaning against hers for support, I felt her fingers grazing between the lips of my pussy, and then they were gone again.

"Follow me," she said, placing both our drinks back on the counter.

18

I noticed her give the bartender a nod, to which he responded with a wink. I felt awkward and embarrassed (did she do this often?), but I also wanted her fingers back inside me as soon as possible.

I followed her toward the women's bathroom. At this hour of the night, it was deserted. She glanced at the open cubicles before choosing the larger, handicapped one. I walked in beside her, scooting to the side as she latched the door shut. Turning, she pushed me against the wall, lips suddenly against mine, fingers on my already aching nipples.

"Take your pants off," she told me, already unbuttoning her own.

In a matter of seconds, two pairs of jeans were draped over the hook on the back of the door, and we stood facing each other just in our tops and underwear. While I watched, she unfastened her bra, slipping it out from under her shirt, and tucking it inside one of the pockets of her pants.

I heard the outside door open, the sound of music temporarily blasting through the room, replaced by the sound of someone using the adjacent stall. I looked at Natalie, suddenly self-conscious and unsure of what to do next. She merely brought her index finger to her lips.

"Shh…" she whispered before stepping closer, taking hold of my underwear with both of her hands and tugging it down with one quick move.

Just like that, my panties were at my ankles. I stared at her. I thought about doing the same to her, but I was enjoying letting her take charge. I could feel myself aching to be touched, and I tilted myself toward her as I leaned my upper back against the stall of the door. As if on cue, our quiet neighbour washed her hands and left us alone again.

With a smile, Natalie bent down, gently resting her knees on the tile floor. Even though part of me wanted to watch her, another part of me still felt hyperaware of the awkwardness of the bathroom environment, and there was a safety to leaning my head back and closing my eyes. I rested my hands on her head as she came in close, the tip of her

19

tongue flicking over my clitoris, perfect little circles that sent me swooning, alternating with longer licks than ran one from end of my pussy to the other.

Her tempo changed, speeding up and slowing down, while I could hear myself moaning, my fingers grabbing her hair even more tightly, the smooth wetness of her tongue running over the swelling heat of my insides, back and forth, round and round, and then suddenly there was a finger tracing circles over the entrance to my pussy, and that was what did me in, with one great wave of throbbing and sensation, still leaning back against the bathroom wall. After a couple deep breaths, I opened my eyes and looked down, her lips glistening with saliva and the wetness of my own body. She smiled at me, and I smiled back.

What do you do next?

Give the bartender your phone number?
(turn to page 69)
or
Invite the bartender to come home with you?
(turn to page 72)
or
Keep hanging out at the bar with her?
(turn to page 74)

Her place

There was a limit to the amount of progress any interaction could have in a bar, and not only because of the noise and surrounding people. There was something undefined which only happened when you went to someone's home, when you spent time with them between their four walls, and if she was ballsy enough to invite me to hers, there was no way I would turn that proposal down.

"Let's go to your place. That sounds great."

She smiled at me, and I said goodbye to my friends while she got the rest of her things from behind the bar.

"Ooooooooh, girl, don't do anything I wouldn't do," Sarah said, laughing and grabbing my ass.

I jumped away, hoping Natalie had not noticed. I was still feeling dumb and nervous about the whole thing.

"Shh!" I whispered. "Don't embarrass me!"

"We would never embarrass you. At least not on purpose!" Rachel grinned. "Come here, have a goodnight hug."

I stepped over and gave her a quick hug. Natalie was waiting, and I was anxious to get out of there. I did not want her to reconsider her invitation.

I gave Laura a quick goodbye kiss on the cheek, as she told me "Good luck" under her breath. I smiled at her, turning to leave.

"Your car or mine?" Natalie asked. "Or should we just drive separately?"

"Separately is probably better. That way we don't have to come back here—later." I almost said "tomorrow" but then caught myself just in time. I had no idea what to expect from the next couple hours, and if they would translate to a sleepover or not. I did not want to make any assumptions, and I certainly did not want Natalie to think I was getting

21

clingy.

"Sounds good. Follow me!"

I got in my car, turning to look around for hers. She was already waiting by the exit, in an adorably hot red Mustang convertible, and I thought fleetingly that I had never been in a convertible. Perhaps, if tonight went well, there would be an opportunity in the near future. I grinned at the prospect, my mind already coming up with delicious scenarios.

She did not live far from the bar. It was just down the main street, and then a quick left, and another right, and we were there. I parked behind her and got out of the car. It had been so long since I had been in a situation like this one that I felt incredibly naïve and inexperienced. I kicked myself for not keeping a little Ziploc baggie with toothbrush and toothpaste in the car, but I did not, since one-night stands were not the norm for me. I just smiled and said nothing as I followed her up the path to her apartment building. I tried to act cool.

Natalie's apartment was small but cute. Potted plants littered horizontal services, a large decorative fabric hung on the front wall, and I could see a multi-colored lamp hanging over the dining room table. The living room walls were painted purple, and there was a large dog asleep on the couch.

"His name is Akira," she said to me, looking over her shoulder as she headed into the kitchen. "Can I get you some water?"

Akira opened one eye and peered at me lazily. I gave him a scratch on the head before following her into the kitchen. "Water would be great."

Standing in the small kitchen, even without trying, we were practically hip to hip. When she turned around from the refrigerator door, letting it close behind her, I was right there, and when she handed me my glass, our fingers touched. For a second that felt longer than a second, we were both holding the glass, looking at each other. I was surprised that neither of us dropped the glass since it felt like neither

22

one of us was actually holding it. If this had been a movie, the glass would have floated away or dramatically shattered on the floor, but since we were not in a movie, the glass was somehow passed to me, and I held on to it, her hand dropping back to waist-level.

Suddenly, the water did not interest me anymore. Barely glancing to see where my hand was going, I shoved the glass onto the counter, stepping forward to push her up against the refrigerator, magnets and pictures falling to the floor. She slid her hands around me and under my shirt, pressing against the curve of my lower back to pull me closer. I slipped my right hand inside her pants, using my left hand to unbutton the top button and jiggle the zipper open. Her underwear was red, lacy, and small, but I did not care about it any more than I had cared about the water. I wanted what was inside it.

My right hand brushed over her freshly shaved pubic hair, slightly prickly but satisfyingly shorn. I always liked it when girls groomed themselves, getting hair out of the way of the real business. In contrast to the roughness of her outer skin, the inner skin was blissfully soft and completely wet, and, as I pressed my hand against it, it felt like silk.

She curved against my hand, and I felt myself going deeper, her hips pressing into mine. I leaned over to grab her left nipple between my teeth. She moaned, her arms falling back away from me, against the refrigerator, sending more magnets and newspaper clippings to the floor. She began to move rhythmically against my hand, her movements echoing mine, and I closed my eyes, lifting my head up and resting it against the refrigerator. The plastic felt cool against my skin. Her head tilted toward mine, and, even in my daze, I noticed the softness of her hair on my face.

I kept pressing my hand against her insides, up into her pussy, my thumb on her clitoris, sliding in and out, imagining my hand as a hard cock splitting her open from the inside out. I slowly picked up speed, and the weakness in her knees, as she leaned against me and the refrigerator, was

23

the perfect indication that I was doing something right. And then the rug beneath us gave out from the pressure, sliding toward the stove, and we both fell, laughing, to the floor.

She used that as a cue to reciprocate, to unbutton my pants, exposing my black, not lacy but still small, underwear, slipping her hand between my legs. I never liked it when girls did each other simultaneously. I preferred to concentrate on one, than the other (meaning first her, and then myself in this case), and I twisted my hips to the side, shaking my head, a slight grin on my face.

"You'll have to wait. I want to finish you first."

She laughed, slipping her hand out from between my legs and lifting it obediently over her head.

"I can't argue with that, can I?" she said. "Please continue. I'd hate to interrupt you."

Smiling, I placed her left hand above her head, beside her right, and continued where I had left off, only, now that we were horizontal, I had some added encouragement to tug her pants down to her ankles, giving myself a full view of the beautiful triangle of red lace framed between her hips. It seemed almost a shame to take them off, but only *almost*.

With a quick tug, they slid neatly down to her ankles. She stared up at me, her mouth open and inviting. I bent over to press my lips against hers and, with my tongue exploring her mouth, I ran my hand over her bra, across her stomach, and back between her legs.

From this position, with her pants and underwear banished to her ankles, it was much easier to get my fingers inside. Lips against lips, tongue caressing tongue, teeth tapping teeth, we made out above the neck like high school lovers, while I fucked her beneath the waist like a porn star. My fingers, covered with her wetness, slid straight and deep inside her. I could feel her sigh in my mouth. I shoved first one, then two, fingers inside her as far as they would go, feeling them curve along the edge of her body, pressing into the hot flesh of her insides, moving back and forth along the slippery soft skin, in and out, slowly, making her drip over

24

the linoleum, rubbing steady circles with my thumb over her clitoris.

The more I rubbed and the deeper I pushed, the more her mouth devoured mine. Using a careful exercise of balance, I adjusted myself so that my left hand could reach inside her bra, finding her nipples and rubbing them, first one and then the other, pinching them, ever so slightly, while she moaned again and bit my lower lip. My face was starting to flush, but the last thing I wanted was for her to touch me. I was using everything I had to concentrate on her, to sense her rhythm, to coax her closer and closer to a climax. My nipples felt as hard as hers, and my clitoris nearly as swollen.

I stopped moving my fingers, resting them inside her while I began to rub her clit in earnest—round and round and round—as she stopped trying to devour my mouth with hers, tilting her head back on the floor, exhaling with sharp, little breaths that grew faster and faster. Her thighs tensed up as she started to come, and she grabbed my left arm with her right, clenching it tightly, the moans getting louder and louder until, finally, there was a release. I could feel the throbbing of the blood-filled veins in her pussy. I left my hand in there for another minute longer, not moving, just watching the pink on her cheeks, her eyes closed in a state of bliss. I smiled. She looked beautiful.

Opening her eyes, she looked at me and gently slipped her body off my hand. Tapping the floor beside me, she gestured for me to lie beside her on the cool linoleum floor. I willingly obliged, nestling beside her, my head on her shoulder, her hand holding mine. Even though I had not come, I felt as relaxed and satisfied as if I had.

We both lay on the floor for a couple minutes, as though it were perfectly natural to lie on linoleum floors in the wee hours of the morning, until a drowsy Akira stumbled over and stuck his wet nose in our faces.

Natalie laughed, shoving him aside.

"I've got to take him for a walk," she said. "We can walk you down to your car, if you like?"

25

Hmm. I was being dismissed. Okay. Maybe that was for the best, anyway. Good to take it slow. I nodded, getting up to retrieve my clothes. The two of us dressed quickly and silently, early morning sunlight starting to come through the windows.

Part of me kept shouting to myself, STAY STAY STAY, which was why I was all the more startled when she said, "Oh. It hadn't even occurred to me. Maybe you'd like to stay?"

I had one of those moments where you wonder if the voice in your head actually came out of your mouth, but I knew I had not said anything. Maybe the look on my face was just that transparent?

"I can clean the dog hair off the bed. You can stay if you like," she added.

There was a questioning tone to her voice, but I was not sure if it was because she was hesitant about me spending the night, or if it was because she could not tell what I wanted.

So what do you do?

Sleep on the dog hair sheets?
(turn to page 78)
or
Play it cool and go home?
(turn to page 109)

26

Home

I knew I should probably go home and say goodbye to my friends, but saying goodbye to those girls was never a short affair, and my situation was desperate. If I did not get home within the next few minutes, I would end up gyrating against my stick shift or something equally porn-worthy. At my first red light, I texted Rachel to tell her that I had had to go home, and that I would call her tomorrow. She was the most phone-obsessed of the girls, so I knew she would be checking her phone, and then she could pass the word on to the rest of the girls.

Sure enough, she texted me back thirty seconds later with a wink and "Have a good time." Clearly she thought I was heading back to my place with the boy. Ha. Little did she know that he was currently speeding home on the 101, further and further away from me with every minute, while I was going home to satisfy myself with a much less complicated (but much less satisfying) package.

It did not take long until I pulled into my parking space, and it was only moments later that I was readying myself for some satisfaction. My preparations were both simple and specific. My vibrator was loud (as most battery-powered ones are), so I preferred to wear earplugs, as they made it easier for me to distance myself from the machinery between my legs, focusing more on my own imagined scenarios. I slipped them in, grabbing the KY on the way to my bed.

My jeans came off first, followed by my underwear. I dropped them on the floor beside my bed. Lying down, I squeezed a small amount of lubricant on the tip of my dark purple vibrator. Soon, soon, soon, I thought. Adjusting the pillows behind me, I spread my legs and slipped the vibrator between them. I twisted the dial on top, turning the power about three quarters of the way up, just where I liked it. The

27

plastic tip grazed my clitoris with a satisfying vroom, and I began moving it in slow and repetitive circles. My eyes closed, I let my imagination take me to a place where men did not disappoint, and I could control exactly what happened.

My current favorite fantasy, which seemed to do the trick consistently, was as random as many of them often were. I remembered the ridiculous one that was en vogue for me a couple years ago, involving the guy who paid to rub my feet and did my dishes with a massive hard-on. There was also the one where I seduced my boyfriend's younger brother one night after running into him playing computer games, knowing that he had been spying on my boyfriend and me having sex.

In this one, however, I was a massage therapist. For the sake of topicality, I decided to let my ex be the client. Of course, as fantasies and dreams go, exact details were never crucial, and in this fantasy his face was often blurry, being as I was more concerned with other areas of his body, and my breasts were bigger than they really were, so that they could dangle more conspicuously in front of his face.

The fantasy started out with him lying on my massage table. He was naked, except for a sheet covering his "private parts" to convey an element of respectability. I walked in the room, greeting him with a perfunctory hello. We did not know each other. This was just a job, like any other.

I was completely hot (of course), wearing, for some reason, a French maid style outfit, with a very fitted waist and tremendous support for my breasts, making them jut out shelf-like. The low-cut top made sure that almost all of my entire breasts were exposed, a thin line of lace the only barrier between me and nipple exposure. The skirt was short and poufy, sticking out to accentuate my ass and the very short distance between the end of my skirt and the tops of my thighs. I was wearing the typical French maid/sexpot high heels, which put me at the right height to lean over the massage table, and also made my legs look like they went on

28

forever.

Standing by the table, I observed his body like a specimen before beginning the massage.

"Have you ever had one before?" I asked.

"No," he replied, doing his best not to stare at my breasts.

I smiled, rubbing some lotion on the top of his chest and his shoulders, making it very hard for him not to see the full curve of my cleavage as it pressed against the tight support of my top. Starting with his shoulders, I made my way slowly down his arms, lingering at each finger before finishing with a slight tug. One, two, three, four, five on the left. One, two, three, four, five on the right.

Next, I tenderly rubbed his wrists and his lower arm, extra lotion applied at the elbows, and then back to the shoulders. Caressing the ridges along his clavicle, I turned my attention toward his chest. A slight grazing contact with his nipples was enough to make them start to harden, something I was quick to notice. His eyes stayed closed, though, and there was no sign that anything out of the ordinary might be occurring. Unfortunately for him, he could not see the smirk on my face.

After "accidentally" hardening his nipples to my satisfaction, my hands began heading toward the lower half of his body. There was not much to do with his stomach; I was more concerned with the pelvic region. Applying more lotion to my hands, I began to turn his hips into glistening flesh, reaching under the fabric that still demurely covered his private parts. As expected, the fabric began to rise. I could see the concentration on his face, the slight tightening of the forehead, as his fingers began to clench into fists while he struggled to maintain composure.

"Don't worry," I whispered, as I gently rubbed his hands until they relaxed. "It's okay."

He briefly opened his eyes, noticed I was watching him, and then closed them again.

Satisfied that he was not going to try to fight it

29

anymore, I decided to switch to his toes. Beginning with the base of his feet, I slowly, thoroughly, made my way up his right leg. The closer I got to the top of the leg, the slower I moved. I massaged deeply, lightly, back and forth, letting the lotion drip over my fingers as I coated his skin. By the time I got to the top of his right thigh, there was not much point for the "professional" fabric. His hard-on was perpendicular to the massage table, and the fabric had fallen off to the side. I let it sit there. There did not seem any reason to move it, and maybe it would make me seem a little more innocent about the proceedings.

Time for the left leg. I repeated the same process, refusing to allow myself to move off the legs, taking every moment to rub the lotion deeper into the skin, to rub circles and ovals and curlicues over his flesh, feeling the strength of the long, lean muscles, as I watched the skin grow shiny under my hands. With his eyes closed, I felt safe staring at his erection, at the way the blood veins pulsed as he grew even thicker and harder, inches away from my hands.

I still refused to touch, his obvious desire making me all the more stubborn. Rubbing his thighs, I let my hands slide down his inner thighs, across them, basically everywhere above, beside, and beneath the one area where he really wanted me to go. I was curious if he would say anything, or if he was docile enough just to lie there and let me do what I was being officially paid to do.

After a while, my impatience grew the best of me. He was obviously very well behaved, and with, the exception of his gorgeous swollen cock, there was no sign that anything untoward was happening, which meant I had to make it happen. As if I did this kind of thing all the time, I put a little more lotion on my right palm, smoothed it around to make my fingers totally smooth, and then I gently wrapped my hand around his balls. Immediately, his legs tensed, although, interestingly, he still did not open his eyes.

"Shh," I whispered, leaning over so that my breasts grazed his chest. "You've got a lot of energy stored up here,

30

we need to shift it a bit..."

I kept rubbing gently, my breasts still grazing his chest, my face near enough to his that I knew he could feel my breath.

"You really should make an effort to rub this area whenever you masturbate, just to keep the circulation moving. A lot of men get stagnant here..." I let my voice trail off as my hand kept up its rhythm.

Without relinquishing any of the motion, I took my thumb and pressed lightly at the base of his cock. He moaned slightly, and I started moving my hand in neat little circles, much like I was doing with my vibrator between my legs. I could feel my clitoris pulsing in tandem with the pulsing veins around his cock. The nice thing about fantasies was that everything could sync up perfectly.

I straightened up so that my breasts were no longer on his chest, but I was still watching his face intently. His eyes were closed, and there were furrows of concentration along his forehead.

"Does it feel good?" I asked.

"Oh my god, it feels amazing." His eyes fluttered open to look at me for a moment before closing again.

The silence hung between us. I waited to see if he would say anything else. He did.

"Do you think you could...oh, never mind."

"What?" I asked, oh-so-innocent.

"It's just that, it would be amazing if you could, I would love it if..."

"Yes? You've got to tell me if you want me to do it."

His eyes still closed, he continued, "...I am sure this is against the rules, and I'm sure you don't do this kind of thing, but if you could, if you would just rub me a little, it would feel so amazing. I would love it."

"You mean, rub you on your cock?" I asked with a tone of cheerful professionalism as if he had requested a little more attention on his shoulders.

"Yes." He paused. "I'm sorry. I realize it's wildly

31

inappropriate."

I laughed slightly. "Yes, that's true." I laughed again. "But I can't imagine it would hurt if I just rubbed a *little*."

"Oh, that would be great!" he exclaimed with relieved exuberance.

"But just a little," I cautioned. "No happy endings here!"

"That's okay, that's okay," he said, the words falling all over themselves. "Just a little would be so nice."

I smiled, both within the fantasy and without.

It was not a big leap from where my hands were to where they were going. With effortless professionalism, my left hand reached over to take over from my right, and my right hand, coated with a fresh layer of lotion, gently gripped his cock with one complete motion. He moaned again, louder this time, and I grinned. My hand, slippery and smooth, slid up and down his cock, also now slippery and smooth, coated with a mixture of lotion and pre-cum.

He got even harder as my left hand made circles around the base of his cock, gently massaging his balls, while my right hand began the usual assembly line motion of up/down. It was when I slid my left hand beneath his balls, the tip of my left index finger reaching into the crevice of his ass, that he moaned, and white cum oozed out of his cock and all over my right hand.

Again, with the perfect synchronicity of fantasy, this was also where I came, the vibrator pressing into my clitoris, waves of vibration running up and down my legs, and I, too, moaned, curving my pelvis toward the battery-powered machine.

With a sigh of satisfaction from a job well done, I switched the dial to off, and rolled over to go to sleep. After a scene like that, I always knew I would sleep like a baby.

Which was exactly what I did, until the next morning, when I was awakened by the beep-beep of my phone. Text message.

"Can't stop thinking about you. Want to meet today?" it

32

asked.

I stared at the phone number, knowing I should recognize it, but I had no idea who it was. Then I remembered the night before, and blushed as I also remembered the fictitious events that followed the actual ones. Now I knew why the number looked familiar and also why it was not entered into my phone. I had erased the entry when we broke up. Now my ex wanted to meet, and I felt strangely exposed, as if he knew what I had done to him the night before on the massage table.

Still staring at my phone, it beep-beeped again. I clicked to read the next message.

"Just finished the new paintings. Want to come see them?"

This one *was* from a number entered in my phone. Andrew. A boy I had been obsessing over since school started. I had been trying to get him to notice me for months, and I had only managed to strike up conversation two weeks before, at an art show. I had told him I wanted to meet him to see more of his work, and he had seemed agreeable about letting a perfect stranger into his studio, provided I waited until he finished the ones that were currently in progress. At the time, I could not tell if he was blowing me off nicely or being genuine. Apparently, I had underestimated the situation. He really *did* want me to come visit. So it was true—when it rains, it pours.

What do you do?

The ex?
(turn to page 38)
or
The artist?
(turn to page 47)

33

Back to the bar

With a sigh that combined irritation and frustration, I headed back into the bar. I did not know why I was still such a sucker for a boy who continually did not give me what I wanted, but I had finally had enough. If Max was going to walk away from me now, I had nothing more to say to him. Chemistry was rare enough, and I knew that if I felt it, he was feeling it to—so if he still got in his car and drove away, well fuck *him*.

Empowered and determined to get at least some action tonight, I made sure to give the hot bartender a wide grin as I sat back on my stool.

"So…?" asked Rachel. "What did we miss?"

"Yeah! What did we miss?" Sarah grinned at me naughtily. "A little quickie in the parking lot?"

I shook my head. Their faces dropped.

"What do you mean? Nothing happened?" exclaimed Laura.

"Shh!" I gestured toward the bartender who, luckily, was slicing lemons at the other end of the bar and was, hopefully, out of earshot.

"Tell. Us." Rachel's whisper was Bette Davis dramatic.

"Okay, okay," I said, "but you're not going to happy. Nothing happened. We had amazing sexual tension, and then he just drove away."

"WHAT?" Sarah practically shouted.

"Yeah." I sighed. "We had one of those kisses, and then 'I think that's as far as we should go tonight.'"

"You're kidding. He said that?" Laura shook her head.

"Sadly, yes…" I took a deep breath. Time to get this drama behind me.

Rachel slipped her hand over mine, looking at me compassionately. "Are you okay?"

34

Nodding, I said, "I'll be alright. But you girls have got to help me make the most of this evening!"

I looked at the bartender. They all smiled. They knew what was going on.

"You got it, lady," said Rachel, giving my hand one final squeeze.

Laura leaned over to give me a hug. Over her shoulder, I could see the bartender watching us, and I made eye contact right back. Time to get this party started.

Turn to page 12.

Meet the ex

I figured, what the hell? Seize the moment, right? He was clearly interested. He was also clearly captivated by my cleavage. I had seen the sexual frustration all over his face and felt it between his legs. I knew he would be going straight home to jack off, so why not participate?

Max was long gone by this point, but I remembered well enough how to get to his house, so I got in my car, turned the engine on, and made my way to the freeway. I turned the radio to Power 106 ("where hip hop lives"), one of my favorite stations, and started grooving to Akon and 50 Cent. There was nothing like a hip hop groove to get me moving, at least in my car when no one was watching, and there was nothing like a fat bass groove for making me feel sexy.

By the time I had pulled off on the Santa Monica Boulevard exit, I was ready for some serious action, and I had been enough of a dork to sing all the lyrics to "SexyBack" along with Justin Timberlake.

His car was in the driveway, and the lights were still on. He was home, and it looked like he was watching television. Perfect. I did not mind a little seduction responsibility, I thought, as I rang the bell. I heard him get up from the couch, and my stomach did a little flip, tightening a bit with nervousness.

But my grin fell off my face when I saw his expression.

"What are you doing here?" he asked, his tone not exactly friendly.

"What am I doing? I, uh, thought maybe I could surprise you, and, uh, we could...finish what we started?"

I made as if to step into his house, but he did not move. I looked down, to confirm that his feet really had not shifted, before looking up again at that terrible expression.

36

"We *are* finished. I'm tired. You shouldn't have come over."

I stared at him, confused. The openness that had been there earlier was gone. His face was cold. Everything about his body exuded closure. We were finished. *Really* finished. What had happened earlier was a mistake. Or, maybe, if it not a mistake, a fragile beginning to something I had just stomped all over.

"I'm sorry," I whispered, turning to leave.

He said nothing, making no move to grab me or prolong the moment. Tears welling up in my eyes, I rushed back to my car. I had made a terrible error of judgment, and now our relationship was really over before it had even began. Driving back to my side of town, I hit the steering wheel over and over again. Even Power 106 could not make a difference. I had been an idiot, and now it was too late to talk to the bartender. What a fucked up Sunday.

You lose. Better luck next time!

The ex

The artist could wait. I had been waiting six months for a chance to kick it with my ex, and I was not going to wait a minute longer than I had to.

"Yes. Today would be great. When?" I texted back.

"Lunch? Thai? I'll pick you up at two."

Thai. Hmm. Well, he was a creature of habit, and I certainly had no right to be surprised by his selection. We had eaten Thai often when we were together. At this point, though, food was the last thing on my mind, and I was half-tempted to tell him so, but I also knew that playing it cool had served me well so far, so why mess with formula?

"Perfect. See you then."

I had plenty of time to take a long bath and still be able to dress leisurely. I wanted to make sure I looked amazing, so amazing, in fact, that food would also be the last thing on *his* mind. While letting the bathwater run, I evaluated my closet. What should I wear? What was demure enough for lunch but sexy enough for after?

I settled on an airy, see-through pink top that fit snugly over my breasts, giving the illusion of almost post-pregnancy sized breasts, but was also soft and feminine enough that I did not come off slutty. I would wear it with my favorite sexy pair of low-riding jeans, a distressed gray pair that had been given to me by a guy I had dated in the fashion industry. Our relationship had gone nowhere, but it seemed an acceptable price to pay for an incredibly hot pair of pants.

Satisfied, I returned to the bathroom, which was steaming up nicely. Since I had plenty of time, and lots of anticipation, I decided to make the most of it, lighting a couple candles and throwing in some lavender bath salts. By the time I stepped into the tub, with the right amount of imagination, I felt like I was in a spa. I closed my eyes,

38

dropping my head behind me into the water, feeling the warm liquid envelope and embrace me, my hair drifting over the surface. I felt the incredible thrill of both a good night's sleep and the anticipation of a very satisfying day.

That thrill naturally led to a tingling between my legs. I debated for a second whether to reach down there—or if to maintain the sexual frustration a little while longer, leaving me even lustier. I decided that, since I was never one for patience, and I certainly did not want my hormones getting the better of me over a plate of Pad Thai, I would permit myself to indulge.

By the time my fingers reached between my legs, I was wet inside and out. I started slow, first one finger, and then, after a little teasing, two, pressing along the curve of my body, tilting myself against the edge of the tub, slowly breathing in the lavender-scented air, all my attention focused between my legs. The feeling of the water lapping against me as my hips moved back and forth just heightened my sensations. Glancing down, I watched as the water rose above and around my nipples, little waves corresponding to my body's movements. Captivated, I took my left hand and grabbed my right nipple between my fingers.

The pain from my nipple, combined with the pressure of my fingers inside my body, made me want to drift down into the water, and I let my head go. Holding my breath, lungs full to capacity, I enjoyed the sense of submersion, the feeling of being neither here nor there, almost like I had fallen back into the womb. I pressed in and out, harder and faster, making the water bang on the edges of the tub. Little bits were splashing over the side, but, at this point, I did not care. The tub was not that full, and I could clean up later.

I began alternating, a few seconds on my clit, a few seconds inside my pussy, fingers running over the edge of my clit in concentric circles and then back to my dark, wet insides, as deep and as hard as I could shove. I did not have the concentration to go back and forth between my nipples, so I just held on to the right one as if for dear life.

I felt myself starting to come—my first time underwater—and I took a deep breath, so that my whole body could be submerged. What began as a hint of delicious pleasure quickly accelerated, and soon it was a steamroll of an orgasm, as I kept pressing and grabbing and circling, waves of water lapping higher against the sides of the tub. I kept moving—my fingers, my hands, my hips—and holding my breath until, with one big rush, I exhaled, my head shooting back out of the water, gasping for air with a grin on my face.

Amazing.

I slid back into the water after a quick cursory glance around the bathroom. Not much damage, just a little water on the floor. Now even rubbing the soap over me seemed sexy. I felt both utterly relaxed and still pulsing with energy. Rather than taking care of my sex drive, I had been left with a hunger for something deeper, something *interactive*. Smiling as I got out of the tub, I hoped the afternoon would bring just that.

The top and jeans worked together exactly as I had hoped, and, after a final look of satisfaction in the mirror, I answered the door. He had clearly also put thought into his outfit, and he looked *good*. Max never dressed formally, so his looking good was a combination of planning and comfort, but it always made me happy. Today he had on a black t-shirt with longer striped sleeves coming out from underneath which, although it might have looked punk/ragamuffin on someone scruffier, came off as stylish and edgy on him. He had paired it with slim dark blue jeans that gave him an added nudge of urban sophistication. I grinned inwardly. This fine piece of work was mine for the afternoon.

On the outside, I smiled politely, pretending I had not noticed him check out my breasts, motioning for him to come inside. He smiled, and as soon as he had stepped into my apartment, our awkward formality evaporated, and we fell into each other's arms. It still felt good to have him around me, to rest my head on his shoulder, to smell him, to touch the familiar skin, and to notice him getting hard between my legs.

Despite my earlier activities, I felt as sexually frustrated as I always did around him, but I was not going to let it get the best of me. Not only was I worried that, if we got into bed now, we might not end up doing anything else that afternoon (which would not be a bad thing under normal circumstances, but because this was, in many ways, a first date, I wanted to make sure there was some sort of other activity included), but I also thought it would be better if we had some conversation and anticipation before deciding if we were going to go down this road.

Giving him a little gentle rub between the legs, I said, "I think we should save this for later. Let's go to lunch."

He grinned at me, taking my hand. "Sounds good. Let's go."

Turn to page 42.

41

Lunch

Lunch was both long and satisfying, precisely for its length and its frustration. Acting like teenagers, we could not keep our hands off each other. Groping each other under the table, as well as above, I was surprised that no one complained, given that the restaurant was full of its weekday lunch crowd, but maybe we just reminded everyone of their youth—or maybe they were just ignoring us, being a lot less interested in us than we obviously were in each other. The table, small by restaurant standards, still felt cumbersome and too big, but, in a way, it was a necessary barrier, because if we had been sitting in a booth, we probably would have fucked each other right then and there.

As it was, I slipped my right sandal off pretty quickly after we sat down, keeping my shoeless foot between his legs for most of the meal, exercising my toes over both his cock and his balls. I was protected by my jeans, so he could not get his hands between my legs quite the way he wanted to, but that did not stop him from leaning over to kiss me often, and then running his hand over the seam that marked my crotch.

We watched each other eat spring rolls and Pad Thai, long luxurious sweeps of fork-into-mouth echoing a very different kind of insertion that felt more and more inevitable as lunch wore on. Conversation was made, but it was pretty inconsequential, merely filling the time until more physical contact could be achieved. We talked about his friend Scott, who had recently gotten married, and my friend Rachel's new boyfriend, and something about his windows being replaced, and work I had had done to my car, and a slew of banalities appropriate to midday outings between people who had not seen each other in a while. Conversation was clearly not our primary concern.

At long last, the bill arrived and was paid for. Feeling somehow liberated, we found ourselves standing in the parking lot beside his car, awkward again. To grope or not to grope? We looked at each other, uncertain.

"What now?" Max asked.

"I don't know. My place?"

Pause. "Is that a good idea?"

Why was he asking me? "I don't know. Is any of this a good idea?"

He shrugged, suddenly resentful. I tried to diffuse. "What do *you* want to do?"

He stared at his feet. I kept looking at him, hoping for a sign of what would be the right thing to say. Glancing back up at me, he looked vulnerable, more fragile, and I wanted desperately to hold him. He whispered something.

I leaned forward. "I didn't hear you, can you repeat it? Please?" I asked, strangely afraid of making him close off again.

"I want to be with you," he said.

"Well then, let's go. What's the problem?"

"But I don't want to hurt you." He looked at me, dead-on, serious, for the first time that day. "I'm afraid of hurting you. I'm afraid of getting hurt. I'm afraid of doing the wrong thing."

"Look, Max—at the end of this, someone will probably get hurt. Someone usually gets hurt. But that happens no matter what you do. It's just the way things unfold. Your heart gets broken. But that doesn't mean you never put it out there. You know? You just have to keep taking chances and keep trying things. And maybe things work out, and we get lucky, and no one gets hurt."

I smiled hesitantly, waiting for him to say something. He kept his eyes on me, silent.

"I know. It's scary," I continued. "But I'm not asking you to commit to anything, and I'm not committing to anything myself. I say we just try this. We obviously both want to spend the afternoon with each other, so why don't

43

we start there? Okay? And we'll just see where it takes us. Alright?"

He nodded. I smiled at him, and he smiled back. We got in the car. I exhaled a sigh of relief as quietly as I could, feeling the tension ooze out of my body. I was terribly afraid he would disappear into a puff of smoke, but at least I had him for a little while longer. And the longer I had him, the greater my chances of keeping him around.

We pulled into a parking space near my house and walked up to my apartment, with me leading the way. I reached out to take his hand. Even with all the months that had gone by, his hand still felt familiar, and I turned to look at him. Max grinned at me, giving my hand a quick squeeze, and my heart did one of those little flips. Hooray. Maybe this was going to work out after all?

Opening the door, I stood aside to let him pass by. He entered the apartment, turning to face me. I stepped inside, closed the door, and wrapped myself around him. Finally, we were alone. I kissed him deeply, tasting him, feeling his lips, two things I had craved for so long now. He wrapped his arms around me tightly and picked me up, carrying me into the bedroom. I felt almost giddy, like a fourteen-year-old girl who had just gotten her pony.

He lay me down on the bed and began to remove my clothes methodically. I watched him, silent, revelling in how much enjoyment he was getting from the process. He started with my sandals, dropping them gently onto the floor. Then he unzipped my jeans and carefully slid them off, resting them on the chair by the bed. My top came next, and while that was a little trickier, as he had to lift it over my head, this action, too, was performed in silence.

He looked down at me, naked but for bra and underwear, clearly undecided as to what should come off now. I said nothing, just watching him. He opted for the underwear, depositing my panties on top of the jeans. With utmost care, he rolled me over onto my stomach, hands touching me so lightly that my skin tingled. Seconds later,

44

my bra was unclasped, and I was returned to my original position on my back. He delicately slipped the straps off my shoulders, placing the black lace bra on the chair, as well.

Now I was fully naked, while he was still fully clothed. I waited to see what he would do next.

Max unzipped his pants. A lot less fastidious with his own clothes, the jeans were left where they fell—somewhere on the floor. Then his shirt was unbuttoned and dropped on top of the jeans. I looked at him. I could not wait to touch him. With a quick move, he scooted out of his boxers. I did not even notice where those fell, too mesmerized by the smooth hardness of his cock and by my desire to feel it inside me. I raised my arms up, gesturing for him to get on top of me.

Climbing on the bed, one leg on either side, he was hard, I was wet, and neither of us had any patience for foreplay. He carefully took his cock and placed it just at the tip of my opening.

"Are you still on the pill?" he asked.

"Yes." I paused. "Have you had sex with anyone since we split?"

He shook his head. "Have you?"

"No," I lied.

We looked at each other, one of those intense frozen-in-time moments where you can feel the heaviness of the air and the silence, and then, with utmost tenderness, he pushed his way in. Slow at first—and shallow—but with every thrust going a little bit further, a little bit deeper, a little bit faster. I did not move at all. There was no need to. Everything felt amazing. I started to shift, lifting my legs up, coaxing him further, only he shook his head, and, then, with a sudden movement, he rolled us over so he was on the bottom and I was on top.

"I want to look at you," he said.

I had never felt totally comfortable in this position unless the lights were out, but this was a special occasion, so I figured I could oblige him. It had always turned him on to

45

do it this way, and it felt good for me, too, so I told myself to get over the self-consciousness for a little while. I adjusted my legs so that my knees were bent on either side of his stomach, and I begin to shift back and forth, up and down. He moaned. I smiled.

Reaching his left hand upwards, he took hold of my right breast, gently cupping it so that it still moved, but the movement was contained within his palm. With his right hand, he reached around, positioning his thumb just over my clitoris, where he began to rub steady circles, his pelvis and lower back lifting up every time he pushed in. Our rhythms were perfect.

Even though he had never come this way when we were dating, he began to pick up speed and urgency, his left hand growing tighter over my breast, the circles of his right thumb becoming even more sloppy, but little mattered at this point except for the depth of his cock. I kept arching myself against him as he arched himself against me, the two of us going faster and faster, until, with an ARGH, he rolled me over onto my back, dumping himself on top of, and further into, me, and then with one, two, three, four thrusts, it was over. He collapsed across my body, the two of us drenched in each other's sweat.

I held him close, listening to the pounding of his heart and feeling his breath. We lay there like that for several minutes, until both of us fell asleep, completely intertwined and completely relaxed.

What do you do when you wake up?

Play it cool and get him to leave?
(turn to page 103)
or
Keep hanging out with him?
(turn to page 108)

46

The artist

A night of sexual frustration seemed to have done wonders, so I figured I would let my ex wait even longer. I also did not want to risk stalling out on any momentum that might be going on with Andrew. Any delays might make him lose interest, so I thought he should be my priority for the day.

"I definitely want to see the paintings. When?" I texted back.

Thirty seconds later, two quick beeps and then, "In an hour?"

"Sounds good," I wrote.

That gave me just enough time to take a shower, pick the right outfit, and get over there. I texted back "Maybe later?" to my ex and hit the bathroom.

"Hope you can but if not no problem..." was the message waiting for me when I returned to my room, damp and wrapped in a towel.

Typical, I thought. Responsive in such a docile and passive way. Oh well, I had other things to think about.

I turned to face my closet. What does one wear to a studio visit with a sexy artist one wants to seduce? Tight jeans and a blazer seemed studio visit friendly, but definitely not sexually encouraging. A dress seemed like I was trying too hard, since it was not technically a date. I settled on a polka dot skirt that grazed my knees, a tight turquoise top with a white elastic band that fitted around the top of the skirt, and a pair of very flattering pale pink high heels. It was just casual enough that I could give the illusion that I had "thrown it together," if I had been one of *those* girls (which I was not), while also being obviously flattering. I looked satisfyingly at the way the heels flattered my calves and the top gathered snugly around my breasts before grabbing my

47

keys and heading out the door.

When I got to school, Andrew was already outside, sitting on one of the benches by the graduate art complex, face turned toward the sun.

"Hey," I said, sitting down beside him.

"Hey," he said, turning to face me, his brown eyes squinting in the strong L.A. sunlight.

"Thanks for letting me come and see the new paintings."

"Of course. Thanks for being interested in them."

His eyes searched my face for something, and I, suddenly self-conscious, looked away. I was aware of the potential awkwardness of the moment, and I did my best not to fixate on that, because, if I did, it would translate into my actions. I had to play cool. I needed to make a good impression. With the exception of when I went up to him to introduce myself, this was the only time I had had a conversation with him, and it was definitely the only time I had been alone with him. It was also the first time I felt like I could study his face as much as he appeared to be studying mine.

His hair was a short golden brown and his eyes a dark brown flecked with golden bits. It was a satisfying face, full of warmth and intelligence, but also with a hint of something naughty, an element of the renegade or the troublemaker, and, more than anything, that was the part I wanted to expose and experience.

Andrew got up, heading toward the building's entrance. I followed, unable to help myself from watching his ass in his faded blue jeans. This guy was even hotter now than he had been in all the stolen glances I had accumulated over the past few months, peeks down rows of other students in late night classes, rushed glances across the parking lot, whenever I could catch a glimpse. I had struggled to find an opportunity to introduce myself much like now I was struggling to figure out a way to bridge the gap currently between us. How to transition from an atmosphere of professional detachment to one of mischief and seduction? Sadly, I was at a loss, but at least I was *here*, with *him*, which meant I was on track to something.

"Have you been having a good day so far?" he asked, turning to look at me over his shoulder as he opened the door to his studio.

I smiled. "Yes. At least, for the short time I've been awake, and now here..."

He smiled back at me. "After you," he said, gesturing toward the inside of the small room.

It was the same size as the rest, but it was also immaculate which made it feel grander somehow, the bright paintings on the wall the only elements of color in a space which was otherwise limited to white walls and a dark gray cement floor.

"Sorry it's so sparse," he apologized, "I took all my stuff out yesterday for my mini-review."

"No problem." I noticed that he had pulled two folding chairs to the wall beside the door. "Are those for us?"

He laughed. "Yeah. I grabbed them from the hallway. The problem with sparse is that there is nowhere to sit down!"

Funny guy. I sat down on one of the chairs, trying not to feel prim as I crossed my legs in my demure polka-dotted skirt. I watched him glance at my legs, and I wondered if it was merely a curious glance or a lustful glance. I wondered if he could sense my desire to see the body inside that innocuous black t-shirt and those inconsequential jeans that served merely to tease me with what they were hiding. My demure posture was a total charade. Could he tell?

A small stretch of flesh was exposed between the tops of his socks and the ends of his jeans, which had risen slightly as he sat down, and I had fantasies of taking a pair of scissors and slicing neatly up the seam of those pesky pants. I wanted to tear off his shirt and cut off his pants. I wanted him to stand naked in front of me. I wanted his body to be displayed beside the art, since he was just as gorgeous as his

49

paintings, if not more so. I wanted to look at everything with the eye of the detached consumer for whom everything is potential property.

Still, despite the unacceptability of my thoughts, I smiled in a very acceptable manner, encouraging him to tell me about himself and his art. I heard about his childhood, his crazy relationship with his parents, his sister who raised horses in North Carolina, his accidental placement in art school, the concepts behind his current body of work, his stylistic preferences, his inspirations, etc. If I had not found him so hot (as a person) or so interesting (as an artist), it might have gotten boring, but, as it was, it only felt a little frustratingly formal. I wanted to up the ante a bit, to shake up the dynamic, but I did not know how. I did not want him to feel accosted or dominated, and anything I might do would just feel sadly over-dramatic and/or clumsy. I sighed to myself. I wished he would just dominate me already.

For some reason, Andrew heard my sigh as a cry of dehydration. "Would you like some water?" he asked.

"Sure." I had a bottle of water in my bag, but I was not going to complain. Maybe a walk down to the cooler was exactly what we needed to loosen things up.

We made our way down the hall, around the corner, and through the stairwell to the small kitchen that featured a table, a sink, a refrigerator, and an Arrowhead Mills water cooler. On the walk over, we had again gone single file, him leading the way and me trailing behind. However, as he stood over the cooler, filling up what would be my glass, he reached over and affectionately, possibly even tenderly, grabbed my upper arm.

"Thanks for coming today, Lori," he said. "It's nice to get a chance to talk with you."

I smiled. Our first physical contact. "Thanks for talking with me."

He smiled back, and it seemed like, at last, some of the ice had broken. This time, on the way back to his studio, we walked side-by-side, shoulders even brushing at points. He

50

felt much closer to me, both physically and mentally, and I wondered how close I was to getting him topless.

When we got back to his studio, he entered first. I followed. He closed the door right after I had stepped inside, which meant both of us were standing, side-by-side, virtually against the threshold. Neither of us made any movement to stand further apart. Suddenly, any ice that had remained between us was gone. Now there was only heat.

In the span of the few minutes devoted to walking to the kitchen and back, everything had changed. I did not understand how, or why, but the last thing I was going to do was ask questions. I was too busy staring, at the fine hair along his lip and his chin from a couple days of not shaving, at the pink flush of his cheeks, and the brown of his eyes behind his glasses that made his pupils almost indecipherable.

Andrew stared back at me, although what he saw in my face, I did not know. He seemed to find something there compelling as he reached forward to take hold of my arm, again, but this time it was to pull me toward him. Without saying a word, he gently pressed his lips against mine. I kissed him, wrapping my arms around his waist, feeling the trim warmth of his body, the lithe compactness, and loving it. He was as sweet to touch and taste as I had imagined. There was a tenderness to him that I had suspected existed but had not witnessed.

Sliding my hand inside the waistband of his jeans, I relished the smoothness of his skin, the slight texture of the hair along the small of his back. Now that I had him in my grasp, I wanted him even more. I could feel him pressing between my legs, his kisses covering my neck, my head tilted to the side, staring at the atrium-like covering over his studio. His hands were everywhere, moving as lightly as a hummingbird but sending out waves of electricity that reverberated into the depths of my body. He could not move fast enough.

I wanted to remove my panties, but I did not want to be

51

that kind of girl, so I left them on, waiting for him to take the lead, sending my hands up the inside of his shirt, feeling the muscles taut along his abdomen, the curve of his upper chest, the confident strength of his well-exercised shoulders. I tugged on the fabric, and he got the message. Soon enough his shirt had been relegated to the corner of the studio, and I was soaking in the sight of his naked upper body.

He noticed me staring and grinned back at me. "Your turn."

I laughed. "Why don't you take it off?"

Walking toward me, Andrew reached over and, with luxuriating slowness, carefully slipped my shirt over my head. I stood in front of him in my bra and polka dot skirt, feeling very much like an object on display in the daytime brightness of his studio. The barrenness of the room, and the irregularity of what we were doing, made me feel even more aware of my own partial nudity. If there had been lights to dim, I would have dimmed them, but there were not. We were left, instead, with the uncompromising brilliance of daylight streaming in through the open ceiling, and I felt like I was about to be painted.

I told him so.

He smiled at me. "Want to *really* be painted?"

"What do you mean?" I asked.

"Paint. On your gorgeous skin."

The index finger of his right hand traced my upper arm the way a high-class debutante inspects for dust, only the look on his face was not so disagreeable. It was something else entirely, a look which made me want to take off all my clothes as quickly as I could so we could get to whatever was going to come next.

"You want to paint *on* me?"

"Yes." He nodded, smiling again. "I've never done that before, and I'd really love to try—with you."

"Will the paint wash off?"

"Absolutely. I've got several tubes of water-based paint."

52

"Okay. I'm game. You're the artist. Just tell me what to do."

"All you have to do is stand there, let me take off your clothes, and then let me have my way with your skin."

I grinned. "You got it."

He led me to the middle of the room. Standing me dead center, like a ballerina in a music box, Andrew lifted my arms up, removing my bra with a look of devout appreciation for what lay beneath. I tried not to let on how nervous I was. I kept breathing in, slow and steady, observing the look of tremendous concentration on his face, and the expression of tremendous desire evident between his legs, the fabric of his jeans having grown conspicuously tighter along the crotch.

With the precision of a tailor, he unzipped my skirt, letting it fall to the floor, where he grabbed it and lifted it under first one foot, then the other. I let him adjust my body as he saw fit, so interested was I in the procession of events that I wanted to be as minimally disruptive as possible. He unfastened the buckles of my heels and carefully slipped those off, as well. Just the slight touch of his hands on the soles of my feet was enough to make me want to be horizontal, made my spine want to crumble, letting me collapse, but I held myself together with every ounce of discipline, waiting to see what he would do next.

Once I was fully naked in the center of the studio, my bare feet on the cold cement floor, feeling slightly like a slave up for auction as he scrutinized me, lost in thought, I wanted to joke, "Are you going to check my teeth?" but I kept my mouth shut. This was getting too interesting to interrupt—and certainly not with nervous humour.

Andrew turned toward a small bookshelf in the corner of the room. The shelves did not contain any books. They were, instead, filled with tubes of paint, clean Tupperware containers, boxes of ramen, paintbrushes, and an electric kettle. I smiled. It reminded me of the Rothko quote, that now that he had learned to live off sardines and the

53

neighbor's milk, he had to be an artist. Ramen and paint tubes, indeed.

I could not see what he was doing. I heard him grab a couple tubes off a shelf, but his back was toward me, and all the action was in front of him. I waited patiently and a bit nervously, very aware of my nudity, and the fact that people who were not at all naked were just outside the door. When he turned back to face me, he was holding one of those Tupperware containers, a large flat rectangular one, with four large droplets of paint, each one a different color. He had selected black, red, turquoise, and white. I smiled at him as he walked over.

Looking at me as though I were not actually there, but simply a body composed of parts, his eyes ran over me with a look of detached appreciation, the way one might observe a 1968 Ford Fairlane in an excellent condition.

"With what color are you going to start?" I asked hesitantly.

He looked at me, grinning, like a kid at Christmas, knowing that all his gifts were going to get opened, unsure of which should be tackled first, but appreciating the delight that goes along with excess.

"I don't know, what do you think?"

I looked into the Tupperware. "I would say black or turquoise."

He nodded, contemplatively, his eyes darting back and forth between the two. "I vote for the turquoise."

"Alright. Let's do it."

I spread my arms wide and took a deep breath. I hoped the paint would not be cold.

Andrew smeared his index finger through the turquoise before running a steady line of turquoise Indian war paint across the center of my chest, one vertical line stretching from just above my breasts down to where the tops of the ribs come together. It felt good. It was not cold, just slightly cooler than room temperature, but it felt magically smooth as it sat on my skin, like another layer of glistening vibrant

54

flesh. This shade of blue felt appropriately mine.

He kept going, the whole experience taking on a surreal kind of atmosphere as the layers of paint grew heavier, the turquoise followed by black followed by red, finishing with white. Despite the tenderness with which Andrew applied the paint, there was no real sexual vibe taking place on either of our parts. I felt like a doll being decked out for some bizarre ceremony, and he was clearly nothing more than an artist at work. The last step was a white stripe across my forehead, and then he stepped back to survey his creation.

I did not even think of smiling. There was a gravity to the proceedings of which I was incredibly aware, and I just stared right back at him, some kind of multi-colored peacock-like beast. I felt empowered, as if I had been anointed with black magic voodoo priest status. He stared at me in silence, his eyes running over my body, and then he grinned.

"It's amazing," he said.

"Is it?"

"Oh yes, most definitely. And I know just what we need now. Give me one second."

He opened the door just a crack, peering out both left and right to make sure no one was passing by before slipping out. I waited patiently, still feeling transcendentally calm. It only took him about thirty seconds before he was back in the room, a large white sheet folded under this arm. Giving me a nod to step back, he shook out the sheet, spreading it across the floor.

Once it was flat and arranged to his satisfaction, he looked over at me.

"Come on, lie down."

With a speed I had not yet seen from him, he whisked off his pants and underwear. Before I had even figured out how to lie down, he was naked, sprawled on the sheet. I grinned at him and his extended arms.

"Come on. Let's get some paint on me…" he beckoned.

I laughed, lying down on top of him. His body was as

55

beautiful as I had expected, but getting him dirty was even *more* fun than I had expected. I rolled over, leaving trails of multi-colored acrylic behind me. Andrew grabbed me and pulled me back to the other side, more stripes of color left in my wake. I was getting it all over him and the sheet. I felt like a child just discovering finger paints.

We rolled around together, back and forth, at first just playfully, smearing paint with our hands, our arms, our legs, even our stomachs. Most of the paint was still on me, because some had dried before this part of the game had begun, but quite a lot was coming off onto him. To my enjoyment, the merriment of this exchange finally shifted the serious dynamic that had been lingering since I had arrived.

The playfulness continued, despite the growing desire between my legs and between his. We ended up with me on my back, him above me, arms straight, looking down, his upper body curved as he leaned back enough to get the distance he needed to study me.

"We're quite a pair right now, aren't we?" he said, smiling.

There was paint all over his face and chest, and I could feel the paint drying on my cheeks. The sheet looked like Joseph's Technicolor Dreamcoat. I opened my mouth to reply just as he fell into it, his tongue, his lips, his teeth having no concern for whatever paint might be in the way. Andrew kissed me with a hunger and passion that seemed to have come out of nowhere, and I responded, pressing myself into him as hard as I could, our skin fitting together like matching wallpaper patterns.

And then—"Hold that thought," he said, with a grin, getting up and heading back over to the bookshelf.

He rummaged through some of the acrylic tubes, looked behind the Tupperware and inside some of the smaller boxes, before turning to me with an expression of dejection.

"I don't know if I have any condoms."

"Oh no," I exclaimed, deflated. I knew I did not have any, not being one of those girls who carries them around to

56

mid-afternoon studio appointments.

"Wait!"

He turned suddenly, bending over to rifle through his knapsack. With some strange vestige of propriety, I looked away, feeling odd to be looking at his ass, bespeckled as it was with color from my body.

With the glow of triumph, he turned back to me, holding an unopened condom in his hand. I could not help smiling back at him, enjoying the absurdity of the situation. With a dramatic flourish, he tore the condom package open and, still standing, slid the condom over his very erect penis. I grinned. I was very much looking forward to this.

He stood over me for a second, the achieving conqueror, while I looked up at him, watching him watch me. Then he knelt down, legs on either side, left arm above my shoulder, right hand gripping his cock, slowly moving it back and forth over my pussy, letting my wetness coat the latex and driving me crazy in the process.

I moaned, bending my knees and tilting my pelvis up as signs to him to hurry the fuck up. With a look of total concentration, he slid his way in, slowly, gently, both of us not even breathing in the process. It felt amazing. I wanted more. I started slowly rocking my hips back and forth, and he, after resting his right hand in the corresponding position above my shoulder, began to do the same.

The first time you have sex with someone is usually sub-par. This was anything but. The two of us went back and forth, an easy rhythm at first, just enjoying the sensations, the wetness, the electricity that greeted me at every part along the way. We were both almost completely silent, the only sound the steady inhale/exhale of our breath and the occasional murmur and moan, but we started to get a bit louder as we picked up speed.

Lifting my legs up, I placed them on either side of his head to get my hips higher and to allow him to go even deeper. And deeper he went. We were rocking into each other, paint smearing every which way, the sheet thoroughly

57

wrinkled and crumpled beneath us. I pulled him into me, my arms around his back, my legs bent around his shoulders. We were sighing, moaning, sweaty, wet, his face flushed, mine probably pink beneath the turquoise.

Speed accelerating, breath quickening, we moved faster and faster, my clit being rubbed by the edge of his pelvis, my orgasm rising from the combination of inner and outer sensation. My hands were clutching his ass now, and we could not have been more intertwined. His cock was at bursting point, and I was collapsing, shivering with the waves of orgasm that kept on coming.

Just when I thought I could not take it anymore, Andrew climaxed with a groan I was sure someone else must have heard, pressing himself into me with a shuddering sigh. I kept my arms around him as he rolled over onto the floor, panting, coated with sweat, an adorable line of red paint somehow on his forehead.

We lay there, on what was left of the sheet, holding hands, chests heaving, slowly allowing our rapid breathing to subside, the sweat lightly cooling over our bodies. His hand felt warm in mine, and I gripped it, feeling connected to his whole body through those five fingers. I felt the way those fingers wrapped mine, remembering the way my legs had wrapped his body, and I smiled, the drip-drip of post-sex wetness leaking out between my legs.

I felt satisfied. I turned to look at him. He looked satisfied, too. We grinned at each other.

"We've made quite a mess of things," he said.

I looked down. My body was smeared with paint, and the sheet looked ravaged. His body looked like he had rolled against a freshly painted wall.

"How are we going to get you out of here?"

I laughed. I had not even thought of that. I looked over at my clothes. Not only would they barely cover any of my decorated skin, but I did not want to get paint all over them.

"I don't know. Do you have any ideas?"

"Hm. We could roll you up in a sheet!"

58

"Not this one!" I exclaimed, fingering it. "It would attract even more attention than my naked body." I paused. "Well, maybe not *that* much, but subtle it would not be."

We thought together in silence for a moment, and then he jumped up.

"I got it!" he cried out.

He rummaged in his knapsack again, only this time, instead of pulling out an unopened condom (was I ridiculous that part of me wished he had?), he withdrew a baggy black t-shirt.

"I don't have pants to lend you, but I've got this extra shirt. Will it do?" He lifted it up to his nose to sniff. "I'm pretty sure it's clean. It definitely doesn't smell…"

I smiled. "It will be fine."

Standing up, I took the shirt he so kindly offered and slipped it on. It was not that much bigger than what I might ordinarily wear to bed, and it felt comfortable and lived-in.

"Hey. It looks great on you," he said, grinning at me. "Are you going to steal it?"

Funny boy. "Perhaps," I said, looking over at my clothes to figure out what else I could wear.

The paint seemed to have dried, and so, with luck, the polka dot skirt might survive the trip. I slipped it on carefully, zipped it up, and looked down to inspect myself. I definitely appeared a lot less stylish than I had when I arrived, but at least I would make it to my car without attracting too much attention.

The bathroom, luckily, was just around the corner from his studio, and, after making sure no one was in the hallway, I slipped in there to wash the paint off my face and arms. The paint was water-based, as he had promised, and so it did not take much scrubbing to get it off. I looked at myself in the mirror. I was a little pink from the scrubbing, but not so anyone would really notice.

It was odd, of course, for me to be leaving wearing different clothes than I had shown up in, and to be looking so significantly worse for wear, but I did not think anyone had

59

seen me enter the building, and, if anyone saw me leave, I certainly did not think they would care—much. It was a small department, and I had thought twice before pursuing my crush because I knew gossip would spread like wildfire, but at the end of the day, I did not care, and I certainly did not care enough to override the ridiculous lust I felt for this scrawny painter.

Still looking in the mirror at myself, at my bedraggled hair and my post-sex, post-scrubbing glow, I wondered what I should do next.

What do you do?

Invite the scrawny painter to have lunch with you?
(turn to page 61)
or
Play it cool with the scrawny painter and decide to call your ex instead?
(turn to page 66)

Lunch with the painter

"Hey," I said, poking my head back in the room. "Wanna go to lunch?"

Bent over, he was cleaning up paint off the floor, but he stood up to look at me.

He grinned. "Sure. That's a great idea. I'm starving."

After a quick scan around his studio to make sure all was as it should be, he grabbed his knapsack, slinging it over one shoulder, before stepping over to the doorway. With one arm over my shoulder, he locked the studio door behind him and escorted me down the hallway. We did not run into anyone, so all my fears were unnecessary (as they usually were), and we emerged into the blinding mid-afternoon sunlight unnoticed and unacknowledged.

"No gossip," he said, smiling, as if he had read my thoughts.

"Not yet," I replied, with a smirk, and he grinned in response.

We were on the street, a long line of parked cars on either side. "Mine or yours?" he asked.

"Why don't you drive, then you can surprise me with wherever it is we are going?" I suggested.

"Brilliant idea!"

Andrew stepped forward, and I followed, toward the dark blue BMW two-door that was his vehicle. He opened the passenger side for me, gentlemen-style, and I slipped inside. He made his way around the car, getting in on his side. I smiled at him, feeling a bit like two high school students skipping out on sixth period to go to the mall. He smiled back, stuck the key into the ignition, and away we went.

We did not drive too far, just into South Pasadena, to an ivy-covered Italian place with an open courtyard.

61

"Are you sure you want to go here?" I asked.

"Why not?"

"Well, isn't it kind of hoity-toity? I thought it was a pretty fancy joint...?"

"What's wrong with that? Sounds just right for a girl like you!" He winked at me.

"Isn't it really pricey? And will they let us in dressed like this?"

"You mean dressed like art school students?" he asked, laughing. "Considering that my credit card is as good as anyone else, I'd like to see them turn as away. Plus it's only the lunch menu, so I'm sure they're happy to get the business." Andrew looked at his watch. "I think we'll be after the lunch crowd, anyway, so if we're lucky, they'll be nice and quiet, and no one will pay us much attention..."

With a complicit grin, I took his hand, and we walked into the restaurant together. As if sensing our desire, the waiter seated us in a remote corner, appropriately distanced from bathroom, kitchen, or any other kind of thoroughfare. Peeking at each other over our menus, we both smiled at each other. As Andrew had predicted, no one seemed even to notice us, much less judge us.

Despite the fact that I was not usually a mid-afternoon drinker, the white wine he ordered felt appropriate for the decadent nature of the day. We made small talk as we waited for our food, neither of us terribly interested in conversation. I realized that I barely knew this boy at all, which made it somehow strange that I had grown so obsessed with him, but so love (or lust) goes. For now, the physical intimacy we had shared had served to make me hunger for more, and the more he talked, the more interesting I found him to be.

Andrew moved his chair over a little, sliding my chair closer a reciprocal amount, so that we were seated more next to each other than facing. My skirt was where it was supposed to be, sort of halfway between knee and underwear, but, with a furtive grin, he slipped his hand under the table, taking hold of the fabric, and scooting it up enough

62

so that he could reveal the edge of my underwear, exposing even, to my slight embarrassment, some stray pubic hairs which escaped around the lace edges. I reached to tug the skirt back down my thighs, but he placed his hand over mine, holding it in place. I looked up at him, at his warm smile and the slightest of imploring headshakes, and I let the skirt lie where it was, reassuring myself that, for anyone else, the tablecloth would obscure the view.

Even though the only contact we had was his hand on my hand, I felt myself starting to heat up between my legs, and I spread them slightly further apart, to let in a bit more air. He smiled at me, knowing exactly what was going on. It did not take long before his hand was off my hand and making actual contact with actual thigh, drawing seemingly idle circles across the warm flesh, each circle inching its way further up before heading back down again. By this point, the only thing my skirt was covering was my stomach, and I was grateful for the tablecloth, the empty tables around us, and the laziness (thoughtfulness?) of our infrequent waiter.

It was inevitable that his fingers would discover the dampness of my underwear, that he would trace tenderly the area most probably stained, and that through the thin, stretched-fabric, I would feel his trim fingernail against my clitoris, rubbing against my pussy lips, back and forth, as though scratching an itch left behind by an aggravating mosquito. I felt almost feverish, intermittently cold and hot, heat racing between my legs, chilly goose bumps flicking across my thighs.

I could see the rising temperature also happening between his legs, the geographical transitions as his pants swelled and stiffened, and I grinned as I brushed my hands over his pants, my eyes mesmerized by the desire so transparently turned in my direction.

"Not here," I whispered, as I saw him adjust himself within his pants, watching the moment of deliberation as his fingers hovered over his zipper.

"Bathroom?" he whispered to me, but I shook my head.

63

The restaurant was too small. Anything we did would be too obvious, and the stalls were guaranteed to be uncomfortable. I wanted to wait until the situation was more forgiving. We did the best we could to turn our attentions to our food, which was delicious, my salmon and his pasta almost as sensually decadent as the thoughts running through our minds, everything feeler somehow looser, more heightened, as we made our way through the bottle of wine. We became bolder as the meal wore on, and even though we opted to stay for the delicious chocolate mousse, feeding it to each other bite by bite, the rest of the world had ceased to exist. Our hands were all over each other, and, even though I was getting too drunk to appreciate it properly, I was still very glad the tablecloth existed.

As we left the restaurant, I turned toward the parking lot. Andrew tugged my hand in the other direction.

"Where are we going?"

"You'll see," he replied, with a grin, and I followed obediently. He took me down the street, around the corner, past the Metro station, until suddenly we were in this quiet, obscured little alley, which anywhere else might have been divey, but in South Pasadena was somehow quaint.

He turned to me, pressing me up against the wall. Letting his knapsack fall to the ground with one arm, he lifted my hands above my head. With a complicitous grin, he tugged my underwear down to my ankles.

"Do you mind taking off your underwear?" he asked me, after they had already fallen to the ground, impeding my ankles much as he was impeding my wrists. The question was more a formality than anything else, the smirk on his face rendering my answer thoroughly irrelevant.

He unzipped his pants, sliding his cock not inside my pussy, but simply along the outside, the closeness of my thighs providing just enough heat and friction for both of us to feel a rush of pleasure. I wanted to bend down, to get on my knees, but I could not move. My hands were still above my head, and the sight of his enjoyment was enough to make

64

me keep my thighs clenched together. Somehow, between his pre-cum and my own wetness, there was plenty of lubricant. And somehow, despite the fact that he was not inside me, my lips were open enough that my clitoris was getting as much stimulus as it would from any other kind of contact, and I knew I was getting wetter. His face was starting to flush as he picked up speed.

Just as I was about to suggest a condom, just as the sexual frustration seemed to be driving him wild, I felt my orgasm beginning, and I bit my tongue as my mouth opened with a moan, and I started to shudder against the rough brick wall. I did my best to keep my thighs pressing together, because our situation felt so precarious that any slippage to the left or right would stop my orgasm, would stop his own pleasure. I tried not to move, the quivering rising up my toes, my legs, my whole body, and I started to come. That was all he needed, and he groaned as his cum trickled out over my thighs.

Andrew stepped back, in an attempt to get some of the mess onto the pavement, but it was too late. He was all over me, and I was all over him, and we just grinned at each other, like kids caught finger-painting without appropriate smock attire, and I knew it was definitely time for a shower.

You win—now go get cleaned up!

65

Play it cool

I figured the painter and I had done more than enough for one day, and I did not want to overstay my welcome. Plus, if I left now, I still had time to call my ex. Maybe he would meet me for a late lunch.

After one last passionate kiss, I said goodbye to the painter and made my way back to the parking lot. Luckily, the school was quiet today since we were on a mid-semester break, and I did not run into anyone. Not that I looked that peculiar, but it still made me feel slightly less scandalous. I did not want to be the subject of gossip and speculation.

I waited until I was in the car before picking up my phone and dialing the ex.

Max picked up on the first ring. "Hey."

"Hey."

"Want to have a late lunch/early dinner?"

He laughed. "Sure. Should I come pick you up?"

I thought for a moment. It would be simplest if I met him there, but I liked the idea of us arriving in the same car. It would make it harder for him to leave separately. And I also really needed to clean myself up.

"Sure. I'm on my way home now."

"Okay. I can be there in about half an hour."

"Perfect."

That would not give me much time to shower, but it would give me time, at least, to wash my face, get rid of the paint, reapply a little make-up, and put on something presentable. Sometimes (who was I kidding, this kind of thing never happened, but *still*) I actually enjoyed going from one boy to another, feeling the sweat and smell of the first while in the presence of the second. It was almost like the borrowed testosterone was fueling me, and in this situation, where I felt like my ex was holding all the cards, I

66

needed all the fuel I could get.

I sped home, already planning my outfit, so as to maximize efficiency once I got there. What should I wear? What was demure enough for lunch but sexy enough for after?

I settled on an airy, see-through pink top that fit snugly over my breasts, giving the illusion of almost post-pregnancy sized breasts, but was also soft and feminine enough that I did not come off slutty. I would wear it with my favorite sexy pair of low-riding jeans, a distressed gray pair that had been given to me by a guy I had dated in the fashion industry. Our relationship had gone nowhere, but it seemed an acceptable price to pay for an incredibly hot pair of pants.

The top and jeans worked together exactly as I had hoped, and, after a final look of satisfaction in the mirror, I answered the door. He had clearly also put thought into his outfit, and he looked *good*. Max never dressed formally, so his looking good was a combination of planning and comfort, but it always made me happy. Today he had on a black t-shirt with longer striped sleeves coming out from underneath which, although it might have looked punk/ragamuffin on someone scruffier, came off as stylish and edgy on him. He had paired it with slim dark blue jeans that gave him an added nudge of urban sophistication. I grinned inwardly. This fine piece of work was mine for the afternoon.

On the outside, I smiled at him politely, pretending I had not noticed him check out my breasts, motioning for him to come inside. He smiled at me, and as soon as he had stepped into my apartment, our awkward formality evaporated, and we fell into each other's arms. It still felt so good to have him around me, to rest my head on his shoulder, to smell him, to touch the familiar skin, and to notice him getting hard between my legs.

Despite my earlier activities, I felt as sexually frustrated as I always did around him, but I was not going to let it get the best of me. Not only was I worried that, if we got into

67

bed now, we might not end up doing anything else that afternoon (which would not be a bad thing under normal circumstances but because this was, in many ways, a first date, I wanted to make sure there was some sort of other activity included), but I also thought it would be better if we had some conversation and anticipation before deciding if we were going to go down this road.

Giving him a little gentle rub between the legs, I said, "I think we should save this for later. Let's go to lunch."

He grinned at me, taking my hand. "Sounds good. Let's go."

Hand in hand, we walked down the stairs to the street in front of my apartment building. Max had parked out front, and, like a gentleman, he reached forward to open the door for me.

"Where do you want to go?" I asked, stepping into his car, avoiding the tossed papers at my feet. Keeping his car clean had never been his strong suit, but I was not one of those girls who cared about stuff like that.

"How about Thai?" he suggested, giving a little "umph" as he slid into his seat.

Thai. Hm. Well, he was a creature of habit, and I certainly had no right to be surprised. We had eaten Thai every other time we had gone out when we were together. At this point, though, food was the last thing on my mind, and I was half-tempted to tell him that, but playing it cool had served me well so far, so why mess with formula?

"Sounds fine. We can go to the place you like in Pasadena."

"Great." Max gave me a grin and a squeeze of the thigh, before turning to back out of the parking space.

Turn to page 42.

68

Phone number

I decided that, for once, I would play it cool. I had done enough for one night, and I would act my age.

Busy trying to plot my next move, I did not say anything as we dressed. I was trying to figure out how to give her my phone number in a way that would actually make her want to call. Of course, since life is rarely like the movies, by the time we were dressed, and she was checking her makeup in the mirror, I had thought of nothing clever or flirtatious.

"Here's my card," I offered, striving for a semblance of urban cool as I handed her one of my small red business cards.

Natalie grinned, sticking it in her bra. "I'm gonna keep it there, okay? That way I won't lose it."

"Good." I smiled back at her, disappointed by my lack of game but pleased by her reaction.

"Wait," she said, pulling it back out and handing it to me. "Write me a message on it, okay?"

"A message? What kind of message? So you don't forget who gave you the card?"

Natalie laughed, leaning forward to stroke my cheek with her right hand. "Honey, I'm not gonna forget you. Just write me a little note. Make it a poem. Something short and sweet." She grinned again. "For the memories, okay?"

Okay. I could do that, weird as it was. Grabbing a pen out of my bag, I placed the card on the edge of the sink, and scribbled the first poetic-like thing that came out of my head. "The days are long / But longer still / Are nights without you."

Feeling rather pleased with my off-the-cuff poetic talents, I handed the card back to her. She glanced down at it, her eyes darting over the words. I could see that she was

69

startled and touched by what I had written. Looking back up at me, she smiled, leaning over to deliver a kiss which made my insides melt and sent my clitoris clamoring for more.

"You're a doll," she whispered in my ear, giving my earlobe one quick and sultry lick before sticking the card back in her bra, turning around, and leaving me to make my way out of the bathroom alone.

Squinting a bit into the early morning light, I found my car in the parking lot. Shifting my car into drive, I wondered if I would ever see her again, if she would call, why she had not offered me her number in exchange, and, most importantly, if I should stop off anywhere on my way home. Even though I was not a fan of late night eating, I was pretty hungry, and I decided to stop off at In-N-Out on my way home for a greasy cheese sandwich.

Turn to page 71.

70

In-N-Out

You only make out with a bartender in the bathroom of a dirty club a couple times in your life, if that, so why not indulge the starchy cravings?

But the real deciding factor was the lack of a line. I was able to drive straight up to the drive-through window. To my surprise, the window was being manned by one of the most attractive boys I had seen in a long time.

This was a first. I guessed him to be in his mid-twenties, with soft curly brown hair, brown eyes, and sharply chiselled features. Skater punk meets troubled artist. I wished I had thought to check my appearance in the mirror before pulling up, but who does that in anticipation of an In-N-Out drive-through order? I glanced quickly into my rear-view mirror, enough of a look to see that, while my make-up was fuzzy, my lipstick, luckily, had smudged itself right off, so at least I did not have streaks of red across my chin.

"What can I get you?" he asked.

For a second, I tried to think of something clever to say, before settling lamely for my order. Clearly this was not a night for clever quips. He called my request into the microphone and then turned to face me to take my money.

What do you do?

Decide that he should make the first move?
(turn to page 134)
or
Try a cheesy pick-up line on him?
(turn to page 135)

71

Invite the bartender

"Would you like to come home with me?" I asked her, trying to sound casual, not as though I could not bear to leave her side.

Natalie looked at me for a moment before opening her mouth. I did not know what that silence meant, but the slow inhale which preceded her words could not have been a good sign. It was not.

"Not tonight. Another time."

She bent down, slipped her clothes back on, while I just stood there, sort of staring, disoriented by the lack of sleep, alcohol, and, of course, the heady orgasm. And now she was leaving? I did not know how to process all that. With a quick kiss on the cheek, she turned, unlatched the door, and stepped out. I stayed there, naked, for a couple moments, wondering what had just happened. The whole exchange felt like a dream. I knew that I had not come into the bathroom stall and taken off my clothes by myself, but, once she had left, the bathroom suddenly seemed so much colder, the fluorescent lights stripping away any romance that had ever been in the air. Shivering, I hurried to pull on my clothes.

By the time I stepped out of the bathroom, the main lights were on in the bar, and the cleaning crew had begun to sweep the floors. I squinted, feeling very exposed in the harsh light. Was this the same place where I had spent my lusciously decadent evening? Everything felt faded, the colors cheap, upholstery torn in almost every booth. There was no sign of Natalie. The male bartender glanced up at me, questioningly. Was this the same guy who had winked at us earlier? I opened my mouth to ask him about Natalie, if he knew where she had gone, but then I felt embarrassed. If she had wanted me to know, she would have told me herself.

Dejected and discombobulated, I made my way out the

72

propped exit door. My car was one of three left in the lot. It looked as abandoned as I felt. Oh well. Sunday nights were rarely satisfying.

You lose. Better luck next time!

At the bar

We both dressed quickly, not uncomfortably fast, but in a casual-friends-ready-to-move-on-to-the-next-activity kind of way, as though we had just tried on swimsuits together at the mall. I felt slightly odd about the dynamic, and I wished I could fall into a hole in the floor or automatically disappear to avoid the awkwardness. Natalie, however, did not seem to show any signs of wanting to be rid of me, so why not stay at the bar a while longer and see what happened? I certainly enjoyed her company.

The two of us made our way out of the restroom, a bit more cleaned up than we had been a few minutes prior, thanks to quick glances in the mirror and half-assed attempts to straighten hair and resurrect makeup. Luckily, that late at night, no one really expects you to look anything approaching perfection. Thank god, because I was a long ways from it. My eyes were pinkish, my eye makeup hopelessly smudged, and my skin that post-3 A.M. pale. So it goes.

The cleaning crew had started sweeping the floors, but Natalie did not see that as an indication to leave.

"Come on," she said, motioning for me to follow her toward the bar.

The other bartender was still there, rinsing glasses, and he obviously had a late night crew still going. There were a handful of guys and one other lady knocking down drinks at the end of the bar, near where I had sat with my friends earlier in the evening.

"Hey, guys," Natalie called out as we approached.

They all turned to look at us. I felt slightly intimidated by the rock and roll vibe they were emitting. I was a stranger to this post-3 A.M. world that they so clearly inhabited. I envied the way their fashion complemented their makeup

74

smudges and messy hair (Yes, some of the boys had on traces of eyeliner. Either that or *very* smoky eyes.) While I looked worse as the night progressed, they seemed to grow more comfortable, more glamorous, lizards shifting skins while the rest of the world struggled to fit in.

A chorus of "Hey, Natalie" greeted us, and she turned to introduce me.

"Guys, this is—" her voice trailed off as she looked at me, laughing with flustered embarrassment. "I just realized I don't know your name!"

I smiled, extending my hand to the stylish punks at the bar.

"Hi. I'm Lori."

They all shook my hand in turn, while Natalie put her arm around me affectionately. "Would you like something to drink?" she asked.

I laughed. "I think I've had enough for tonight! Maybe a juice?"

"Cranberry?"

"Yes. That's perfect." I smiled at her, and she smiled back, heading behind the bar to get our drinks.

"Can I get anyone else anything?" she called out, over her shoulder.

The rest of the crowd was clearly not on the juice tip. Gin and tonic, vodka and tonic, and vodka red bull were the requests I made out, as I hesitantly sat down on the first empty stool beside them.

"Who are you?" said the guy closest to me, turning on his stool to face me.

"Who am I? I'm Lori."

"Yes. Yes. I heard that. I mean, who *are* you? What do you do? How do you know Natalie? Are you from Los Angeles? Do you live around here? Those kinds of questions..." He paused, looking at me expectantly.

"Oh." I smiled nervously. I was not used to being put on the spot like this. I had found that the older I got, the more rarely people asked real questions. But okay. I could do this.

75

"I'm a student. I go to grad school for photography and writing. I met Natalie at the bar." I intentionally left out that I had only met her that night. "I moved to L.A. about a year ago for school. Before that I was living in New York, where I had a day job as a graphic designer / web site builder. I live a couple minutes away." Finished, I looked at him, smiling again. "Your turn."

He laughed at me. "Ok. My turn. Let's see...My name is Mark. I'm a sound editor. I met Natalie several years ago, when I was a waiter at a restaurant where she bartended...and...what else did I ask you?"

"Are you from L.A.?"

"Yeah. Born and bred. Spent a couple years in Connecticut with my family but have lived here almost all my life. I love L.A."

People seemed either to love Los Angeles or to hate it. There was not much ambivalence. I was just bending in closer to start asking more questions, when I felt a hand snaking across my back.

"Here's your drink, lady."

I turned as Natalie slid onto the stool beside me.

"Natalie, do you know Mark?"

She smiled. "Yes. Mark's my boyfriend."

I turned, startled, to look at Mark. He was smiling at her.

"Did you have a good night, honey?"

She nodded, grinning. "Yes, thanks to the lady here." She gave my thigh a little squeeze.

I had no idea what to say. I did not know what to do. So I just sat there between the two of them, while they talked across me. At one point, I asked them if they wanted to switch seats, so that they could be closer to each other, but they both shook their heads, telling me to stay put. Natalie put her hand on my thigh again, after that, but this time she left it there.

It definitely felt like she was flirting, but I had no idea how to respond, or what she wanted me to do, or what Mark

76

wanted me to do. At least, he did not seem to be flirting with me—at first. After about half an hour, though, his arm was around me, and he started calling me "darlin'" and I kind of wanted to fall into a hole in the floor. I wanted him to stop, and I wanted her to pick up where we had left off, and I wanted him not to exist.

Then the crew stood up, demanding food. I slid off my stool, wondering the best way to make a quick exit, but this only moved Natalie's attention from my thigh to an arm around my waist. Pulled close to her, we all made our way to the doorway.

"Where do you guys want to go?" asked a girl whose name I had not caught.

There was some discussion of this diner versus that diner versus this bar that served late night food, but I could not make it out because Natalie was whispering in my ear.

"Do you want to get food? Or do you want to come with us?"

"Come with you where?" I whispered back.

"To my place. Or maybe Mark's. His is bigger."

I wanted to laugh. His *what* was bigger? I was still confused as to what, exactly, they wanted with me, but I was starting to figure it out. I had never done a threesome before, however, I had a very strong feeling that this night could be my first—if I wanted to try.

What do you do?

Join the crew for some late-night food?
(turn to page 81)
or
Try your luck with Natalie and Mark?
(turn to page 126)

Spend the night

Even though the dominant voice in my head told me not to stay, told me to go before I was asked to, following the age-old verdict of leave them wanting more, I decided to spend the night. I did not know if it was because I was still feeling semi-vulnerable after the run-in with my ex, or if it was because following the "rules" had kept me single this long, so maybe it was time to amend them. Whatever the rationale, I told her yes—and told myself that I would leave first thing in the morning.

"Great," she said, any trace of real or imagined hesitation gone from her voice. "I'll get the bed ready. Give me a sec!"

With those last words called out as she left the room, I was suddenly alone. It was hard to imagine this same kitchen was the scene of our recent sexual exploit. Grabbing a ginger ale out of the fridge, I leaned against the counter contemplatively. Looking at the fallen magnets and photos as proof of what havoc we had wrought, I grinned, stopping to pick them up. They were the standard fridge fare, photos of Natalie with an older man and woman, clearly her parents, photos of Natalie with a girl who looked like a younger sister, a photo of Natalie in front of the Eiffel tower, a coupon for ten percent off at a local spa—and a photo of Natalie kissing a man.

I could not make out his features too well, since it was a profile shot of both of them, but it was pretty obviously a man, not a woman. Peering closer at the photo confirmed that it was, indeed, a dude, about mid-thirties, with slicked back Rockabilly style hair and a leather jacket. It was a we-want-each-other-so-much-we-are-eating-each-other's faces kind of kiss, without even the glimmerings of platonic-ism to help me casually dismiss what I was looking at.

Just as I was trying to figure out where to put that last troublesome photo, or how to get it out of my mind, if I even should, Natalie walked back into the kitchen.

"Okay, we're all set—Oh…" Her cheerful voice trailed off when she saw the photo I was re-affixing to the fridge.

I turned to look at her. "I'm sorry. I didn't mean to snoop. I was just picking up the ones that fell, and I found it. It's no big deal. I just wanted to put them back up."

I did not know what to say. I certainly did not want her to think I was looking for answers, even though, of course, I was.

"That's my boyfriend," she said, with a neutral tone to her voice, as though discussing the weather. "Mark."

"Oh."

There was a pause, during which I thought of all the things I wanted to say, and a vast percentage of those I could not utter, at least not without my voice squeaking.

She looked at me, as though waiting for me to say something, so I settled on, "Does he mind me being here?"

Natalie laughed. "The only thing he minds is not being invited!"

I grinned at that, which she seemed to interpret as permission to ask if I wanted to invite him to join us. I shook my head. That was most definitely *not* what I wanted. In fact, I was not sure I still wanted to stay.

I thought, with a brief pang, of my ex, and our heteronormative relationship, coached within the reassuring domesticity of monogamy. Did I really want to be here? Maybe I should leave, getting a good night's sleep and avoiding any more melodrama.

Then, again, I *was* already here, the bed was freshly made, and I clearly had a willing bedmate, at least for tonight. So maybe I should stay?

79

What do you do?

Avoid progressive bisexual women and go home?
(turn to page 110)
or
Decide to get in a little more trouble?
(turn to page 114)

Join the crew

"Actually," I said to Natalie, "I *am* kind of hungry. Going to a diner sounds fun."

Natalie looked a let down by my decision. I knew I was probably forgoing any chance of more booty with her, but a threesome with some guy I had just met was not my idea of a good time, so with a feeling of resolve, I stood my ground. At the very least, she made a good show of pretending it was all cool with her.

"Okay. We can do that. And who knows what will happen later, right?" She smiled at me brightly, but it felt a little forced.

Turning to her friends, she asked where they were planning on going. After a brief discussion of diners vs. IHOP, they settled on The Standard, a posh hotel downtown, which served food late, and apparently, had amazing (and reasonably priced) hamburgers. I was not going to complain. In fact, I felt too shy to speak up about anything.

It was too complicated to carpool, so we all ended up driving in multiple cars, an amusing funeral-esque procession fairly undisturbed on primarily empty streets. If only L.A. traffic was as light during other times of the day! It did not take more than fifteen minutes for us all to end up downtown, and, at this hour, we were quick to find parking. The regular bar crowd had left to go back home.

I had been to The Standard before, even stayed there once for a bachelorette party, but I had never visited the restaurant this late. I was surprised that there were quite a few other people there. There were not many late-night restaurants downtown, and certainly even fewer that catered to this nightclub-friendly crowd, so it made sense that they would have a strong pull.

I followed the crew to a big table in the corner, not

81

paying much attention to where we were headed, too busy looking around at the other late night denizens. I could not be sure, but someone looking a lot like Tommy Lee was making out with some blonde in the corner. Trying not to be too obvious, while still quite clearly staring, I almost walked into a chair.

"Oh, sorry," I stammered.

"No problem," muttered a man who looked like Peter MacNicol from *Ally McBeal*, barely turning to look at me over his shoulder.

I blinked twice, walking on, this time practically colliding with our table. It felt fairly obvious, to me, at least, that I was still new to Los Angeles. My life was not glamorous enough to provide regular celebrity interaction, so when it did happen, I was always caught off guard.

I was so out of it that I just fell into the closest seat. Somehow, Natalie was suddenly seated to my right and Mark to my left. I looked first at her, then at him, but they were not paying me much attention, as if they both just happened to sit there by accident, a situation I highly doubted. Punks, I thought, laughing to myself.

I had a feeling they were up to something, some kind of alternate choice of entertainment since I had scorned their more explicit offer. They were determined to get me between them, one way or another. I was curious what they had in mind but felt pretty confident I could handle it, as long as we were in a public place. Even The Standard had standards.

Still smirking at my bad private joke, I reached out to scan the menu as a distraction from my lack of conversational ideas. I glanced it over while everyone talked around me. There were just enough of us that I could get lost in the group, without there being so many that I could disappear and no one would notice. It was a pleasant middle ground, especially considering I was a little buzzed from the alcohol I had had earlier and the late hour. Having to socialize properly felt a bit beyond me.

82

Food was definitely a good idea, I thought, skimming the menu, and I saw no reason to mess with the hamburger suggestion. That sounded delicious, and I was the third person to place the same order with the waitress. Natalie and Mark, both ordering after me, also got hamburgers. It would be a feast of carnage.

The two of them did not pay much attention to me while we waited for our food, conversation drifting this way and that, easy group-oriented conversation about jobs and photo shoots and model scouts. I gathered that one of the girls was a model, one of the guys a model scout for Elite, and two of the guys fashion photographers. That seemed to provide enough conversational fodder for everyone else. Theirs was an industry I knew nothing about, which made it an interesting conversation to observe and less pressing (or relevant) for me to contribute.

"I have to go to the bathroom," Natalie announced abruptly to our end of the table. Everyone nodded dutifully, including me, as if to register her comment.

"Come on, you," she said, tugging my arm as she stood up. "Don't let me go alone."

So much for subtlety.

"Okay," I said, getting to my feet with a slightly self-conscious smile.

The tug on my arm became a grab of my wrist as she pulled me behind her through the tables, behind the man who looked like Peter MacNicol, who seemed to be sharing a piece of pie with an unhappy date, and beside The-Man-Who-Might-Be-Tommy-Lee.

Still distracted by my starstruck nature, I was startled to glance up and see Natalie staring back at me. I blinked. It was a huge mirror just inside the ladies room. I looked a bit worn around the edges, but in that rock and roll way. I felt pleased, like I was finally fitting in. My eyeliner had smudged satisfyingly, and the haggard look was working for me in this light. Natalie, looking hot as always, squeezed my hand, both of us scrutinizing our reflections.

"You're fucking sexy, lady," she whispered in my ear, leaning her head on my shoulder and snaking her hand around my waist so that it slipped in the other edge of my pants.

Still watching us in the mirror, I whispered a thank you back to her.

"Why don't you," she started, as her hand made its way out of my pants and up my shirt, "take your bra off...?" Her hand was now lightly squeezing my right breast.

Feeling a curious sense of disassociation from watching us watch each other, I stammered something about it not being appropriate.

"Appropriate to who?"

"I don't know. The Standard? My shirt's kind of thin. Don't you think everyone will be able to see everything?"

She smiled at me. "What, my dear, do you mean by 'everything?'"

I laughed. That did sound a little dramatic.

"Alright, not *everything*, but you know, full nipple action and all."

"Isn't that the point?" she asked, her fingers tracing circles around my right nipple, causing it to stand out in a very pronounced way, even through the bra. "Is that *your* point?" She laughed at her own joke.

"Come on. Take it off. I wanna see you."

Obligingly, I reached under my shirt to unhook my bra, slipping it off one arm and then another, before pulling it out through the sleeve opening of my shirt. I held it out to her, not sure what to do with it, and she grabbed it.

"Great," she declared, satisfied, tucking it into her pants pocket.

Still not looking at each other, but rather at our reflections, I glanced at my shirt. It was quite sheer without the bra.

"Are you sure it's okay?"

"It's okay with me," she said, pulling me behind her into a stall. "Now I've gotta pee."

84

I leaned against the door while she unbuttoned her pants and squatted, never once taking her eyes off my face, which meant I did not take my eyes off hers, either. Who was I to break eye contact? She grinned at me as she wiped, dropping the used toilet paper into the water. She stood up without pulling up her pants.

"Wanna make sure I wiped?" she asked.

I laughed. "I'm pretty sure you did. I saw."

Leaning over to me, her mouth against my neck, she murmured, "Why don't you check?"

I reached down and slipped my hand between her legs. It was still slightly damp, and just as I was trying to decide what to tell her, she moaned, curving her pelvis onto my hand.

"That feels so good. Press harder."

I slid my index finger inside her pussy, and she grabbed my upper arms with her hands, almost falling into me. As she leaned against me, and I leaned against the door, I kept on fingering her, deep and shallow strokes, in and out, back and forth, until I had had enough with the awkward position.

Getting down on my knees, I lowered my head to the level of where her underwear should been, running my tongue over her cunt, giving special attention to her swollen clit poking out from underneath its hood. The touch of my tongue sent her leaning against the door with a moan that made me wonder if anyone else was in the bathroom, or even *near* the bathroom. But I was too busy to be distracted for long. Circling her clit with my tongue, I pressed lightly enough that she shoved her pelvis toward me, an indicator that she liked it harder.

I gently slipped my second finger inside, my tongue still rubbing its circles. Her legs were pressing against my shoulder, my head firmly between her thighs. The combination of tongue and fingers, licking and pushing, gentle nibbling and sliding, made her moan again, louder, and then once more, until there was a shuddering climax, her thighs squeezing over my ears, pulsing electricity running

85

from her blood vessels to mine.

I gave her a few seconds to catch her breath and then, with a slight squeaking of joints, I straightened my aching knees and stood up.

"That was amazing," she breathed, her mouth barely inches from mine.

I kissed her in response, a long, swooning kiss, as she wrapped her arms around me, and I could feel myself getting wet. She stuck her hand down my pants, pushing just far enough that the tip of her index finger reached the edge of my pussy, and then she pushed a little farther, before pulling back out. Running my finger along her tongue, she grinned at me.

"Yum. You're going to be dessert."

I smiled, watching her pull her pants back up.

"Now let's go eat another kind of meat," she said.

Laughing, she grabbed my hand and pulled me out of the stall.

By the time we got back to the table, the hamburgers had arrived, and mine was sitting neatly in the center of my placemat, looking about twelve inches high. Delicious—and hopefully enough of a visceral pleasure to distract me from the whole other craving that was currently consuming my insides.

The first bite of a hamburger was always the most amazing, when the crunch of the bread was perfect, when the juice of the meat rushed into your mouth, when the flavors blended together, when you were reminded, again, of what a hamburger should taste like. They were right. The Standard did make good burgers.

Apparently Mark agreed with me, because he turned and inquired if my hamburger was as good as his.

"I don't know. Mine's pretty good," I told him.

"Want to taste mine?" he asked, holding his burger in my direction.

I could not imagine that his burger was really that different from mine, but I did not want to be rude, so I said

86

okay.

"Super," he answered, with a grin, only as I leaned forward to take a bite out of his burger, he gave the slightest shake of his head, pulling the burger back toward his mouth.

When I looked up at him, confused, he took a bite, eyes staring straight at mine. Then, mouthful just on the edge of his lips, right between his teeth, he leaned over, gently transferring the morsel from his tongue to mine. There was something hypnotically carnal about the process, and, while I chewed slowly, I could not stop staring into his eyes. The meat *was* delicious, although I could not be sure if it was any different from mine.

As soon as my mouth was cleared, he pointed to my plate.

"Your turn."

"You want to taste mine?" I asked, perhaps a bit slow to comprehend the exchange.

"But of course. It's friendly to share."

Okay. I could do this. Taking what I thought was a small and manageable bite from my burger, I leaned over, this time transferring it from my tongue to his, from between my teeth to between his. Only my bite was not quite as manageable as I had thought, and a small trickle of meat juice ran down my chin and began making its way across the center of my chest.

"Oh," I exclaimed, startled, sitting back and picking up my napkin to sop it up.

Natalie grabbed my arm mid-motion. "Let me do it for you."

Feeling a bit confused by the dual action on either side of me, I only nodded, reaching forward with the napkin to hand it to her. She shook her head.

"I don't need it."

Bending over my chest, she used her tongue, running it from right between my breasts up to the line of my clavicle, and then there was a brief detour left, and then a brief detour right, before going back en route across my neck, to my

87

chin, and then reaching her final destination in my mouth. I was so turned on by this point that I forgot about Mark, much less the people around the table.

We kissed each other, tongue against tongue, so deeply that I thought we would fall into each other, so deeply that, when she put her hand between my legs, it was what I desired while still not coming even close. Curving against her, she pressed harder against the ridge of fabric, against the edge of my bone, against the swelling of my clitoris, and my tongue wanted to devour hers.

"I think it's time for dessert, ladies," Mark uttered softly near my ear but loudly enough that Natalie could hear.

Jolted out of my reverie, I turned to glance around the table. Everyone was ignoring us, occupied with the round of drinks they had ordered, some having moved on to coffee, others still swigging back alcohol. No one seemed to be contemplating pastries.

"Dessert?" I asked. "Are we ordering?"

"It's already been ordered, my dear," he said, sliding his seat back.

I turned to look at Natalie. She was also looking at Mark with a bemused expression, but the hints of a grin indicated that she had her suspicions about his agenda.

"Where are we going?" I asked Mark, taking the offered hand as I stood up.

"We are going to our room," he replied, with a feigned air of elegance. "Dessert will be served there, courtesy of room service."

I turned again to look at Natalie, as if she would have the answers. She was just getting up out of her chair, smiling at Mark.

"Ladies?" he said, one elbow out on either side for each of us.

I took the one closest to me, still not fully understanding. "You got us a room here, in the hotel, for tonight?"

"Yes. I reserved it while the two of you were taking

88

your time in the restroom earlier." He winked at Natalie. "I also took the liberty of making sure ice cream would come a little bit later, and," he looked at his watch, "we should hurry so we are ready for it when it does."

I laughed. This whole evening was getting more and more absurd, but I could not complain. I had had a delicious meal, participated in and experienced lots of delicious inappropriate behavior, and now I was going to see another one of The Standard's famous rooms. All in all, not bad for a Sunday night out.

We took the elevator up to the sixth floor. Feeling a bit like giggly schoolchildren, the three of us ran down the hall, to room 609. Mark opened the door, and we tumbled inside. The room was not as posh as I would have expected from such a trendy hotel, but it was a good size, and the bed and bathtub were both enormous. The bed seemed comfortable for three, and the bathtub large enough for four. Natalie darted ahead, leaping onto the bed.

"It's so big! Come here!"

I laughed at her as she jumped up and down on the clearly sturdy mattress. The bed was covered with little candies that were sent every which way by her movements. I was way too self-conscious to do something as uninhibited as jumping on a bed, so I just leaned against the wall, watching her.

Mark came up beside me, wrapping his arm around my shoulders, and, while also watching Natalie's exuberance, said softly into my ear, "Shall I run you a bath?"

I smiled. "That would be lovely, thanks."

After a pat on my ass, he trotted off to take care of it. I still was not sure what I thought of Mark. I had been guilty of flirting with him before I knew he belonged to Natalie, but now that I knew they were together, I had pretty much lost interest. He had that rockabilly cool which alternated between annoying me and tempting me, since a part of me had never lost its fondness for East Village rocker-types. But I questioned the authenticity of his persona, however, and it left me feeling even more uncertain about what kind of person he really was. He seemed like a lot of posturing.

I knew there was no way I would seek him out on his own, but having him here, supposedly at my disposal, was maybe not so bad. I could try to ignore the posturing if it came with Natalie included.

By this point, Natalie was lying on her back, spread-eagled across the bed. Mark was fussing with the bathtub, adjusting temperatures and inspecting the various bottles of shower gel, shampoo, and bubble bath, so I went to lie beside Natalie. The bed was more than big enough for the two of us to lie without touching, but that would have defeated the purpose of this whole endeavor. I lay down beside her, the back of my neck resting against one of her outstretched arms, my legs over one of hers. We lay like that contentedly, quietly, staring at the ceiling, listening to the water rushing into the tub.

I was starting to drift off when Mark came over to the bed, standing over us.

"Ladies, I hope you're not asleep yet! Your bath is ready…"

I smiled up at him drowsily. He extended both of his hands. I grabbed one, Natalie grabbed the other, and we pulled ourselves up. The tub was not quite the size of a hot tub, but it was definitely longer and wider than a typical bathtub. Looking over at Mark and Natalie, I wondered who would disrobe first. Natalie did.

With one quick motion, she lifted her shirt over her head. Not even looking in our direction, she unbuttoned her jeans and neatly stepped out of them. Next, she unhooked her bra, dropped it to the floor, and her underwear followed. The whole process took less than thirty seconds. With a grin at both of us, she stepped into the tub with the tiniest splash, sending white bubbles cascading off to the sides.

"Oh my god, it feels wonderful," she exclaimed, sliding her body under the water, bubbles hiding everything below her neck. One little perfect knee poked up, like an island

90

among a sea of white foam.

Moving a bit slower, partly due to sleepiness, partly due to shyness, I took off my pants, my shirt, my bra, and lastly my underwear, before joining her in the bathtub. She was right; it did feel wonderful. The warm water had a silky texture, probably due to something Mark had poured into it, and the bubbles reminded me of the carefree childhood I had always wished I had had. Laughing at Natalie, the two of us tossed piles of white foam at each other, while Mark watched, a combination of parent and voyeur.

"Come on in, you dirty bird!" Natalie called out to him. "Stop watching and get in!"

Smiling at us, he reached his shirt over his head, and even I had to admit he was wonderfully built. Lean and muscled, without too much chest hair, and some gorgeous tattoos, I could remember why I had started flirting with him. His jeans joined ours on the floor, and then he, too, stepped into the water.

With the three of us in the bathtub, the water came up close to the edge. Not too close that it would flood the room, but high enough that it covered most of our bodies. This was sad because I had relished the possibility of checking Natalie and Mark out while in this "appropriately naked" situation, but, on the other hand, there was also something thrilling and anonymous about not being able to see or be seen. We were all groping each other under the water without being able to visualize what we were doing.

Mark leaned over and kissed me. Trying to forget that Natalie was right there, I put my arms around him, responding with as much desire as I had felt since he took off his clothes—which was considerably more desire than I had felt while his clothes were still on. As we were kissing, I felt a pair of hands move through the water near my stomach. I glanced down but could not see anything past the white foam. From the look on Mark's face, though, I could imagine where Natalie's hands had gone. She had moved behind him, her chest to his back, her arms wrapped around

91

his waist, while she seemed to be busy moving her hands back and forth underwater.

"I want to fuck you," Mark whispered in my ear, the lines of desire etching themselves into his face, his eyes getting the lusty dog expression men always have when some woman is between their legs.

I glanced over at Natalie, but she was just staring straight at me, a grin on her face. "Go for it," she mouthed at me.

Looking back at Mark, I smiled, giving an almost imperceptible nod. He reached out for me with his arms, pulling me toward and on top of his cock. As he tugged me closer, his cock slid smoothly between my legs. Whatever it was he had poured into the bathwater had become a substitute lubricant. My legs wrapped around him as Natalie made room for the two of us against the edge of the tub. She slid herself behind me, water sloshing over the sides as a result of our movement. Mark was fucking me from the front as she started rubbing me from the back, one hand on my clit, the other on my breast.

It was an overload of sensation; everything feeling like it was at the perfect angle, the combination of all those pressure points overloading my body. I wanted to grip the edge of the tub for some semblance of stability, but Mark begged me to pinch his nipples, so one hand went to the edge of the tub while the other obligingly took hold.

"Harder," he gasped, so harder I pressed, feeling the flesh between my fingers.

I do not know why it always surprised me when men found their nipples as sensitive as women found theirs, but it did. He whimpered, and I released uncertainly, but he just panted "harder" again, so I leaned over, taking his nipple between my teeth, squeezing as my tongue flicked against it.

"Ohhh," he moaned, head tilting back.

I could feel him swell even more inside me—which was impressive considering how big he had been just moments before. His hips jutted forward with a pulsating movement,

92

and my sensations accelerated. He rubbed against what felt like an acute pressure point for me, a place of perfect sensation, the waves of pleasure accentuated by Natalie's fingers circling my clitoris and tugging on my nipples.

I started to moan as I felt myself contracting, my head tilting forward awkwardly, his nipple between my teeth. As I panted against his damp skin, pressing myself even closer toward him, the cries of orgasm seeping out between my clenched teeth, Mark mirrored me, his cock pulsing in time with my contractions, and Natalie's fingers sending my clitoris into paroxysms of pleasure.

I could not stand it anymore. Lifting my head up, I wrapped my arms tighter around his wet body, pressing myself so close to him that Natalie had to slip her hands away from both my breast and my clit, and we came in a mess of turbulent waves against the walls of a bathtub made for four.

What do you do?

Keep hanging out?
(turn to page 94)
or
Decide you've had enough?
(turn to page 103)

Keep hanging out

The three of us clung to each other for a minute more, chests heaving, before slowly disentangling, drifting back to the edge of the tub. Elbows positioned on the rim for comfort, we grinned, full of post-orgasmic euphoria. There was that feeling of false intimacy, of contrived closeness created by shared pleasure. I would have reached forward to hold Natalie's hand, but I did not want to move, and I also did not want to be seen as proactively affectionate while her boyfriend was right there, staring at both of us.

So I just leaned against the edge of the tub, trying to catch my breath. My wet hair stuck to my neck, but I was too lazy to do anything about it.

"Would you ladies like a drink?" Mark asked.

I nodded, as did Natalie. It seemed like the appropriate thing to do in a situation where I had no idea what appropriate protocol would dictate. With a leap of manly purpose, Mark jumped out of the tub, wrapped a towel around his waist, and investigated the mini-bar.

"We need some ice," he reported.

"Are you going to take care of that?" Natalie asked— with a grin in my direction.

"But of course!"

With a flourish as he grabbed the key card, Mark swept his way out the door, towel still around his waist, ice bucket in hand. As soon as he left the room, Natalie lifted her legs, wrapped them around me, and pulled me to her. I laughed as our breasts collided.

"What are you laughing at?" she asked, her eyes sparkling and bright. She was clearly not exhausted at all.

Slipping her fingers underneath my chin, she tilted my face up so we were on the same level. Without saying a word, she leaned over and kissed me. It reminded me

94

suddenly of how this evening had begun, of the intimacy that had started it all before things got complicated, and I happily kissed her back.

Just when I had forgotten he existed, lost in the sweet softness of Natalie's lips, Mark came rushing back into the room.

"Oh my god," he exclaimed. "You'll never believe what I just found!"

The two of us spun around in the tub and stared at him expectantly.

"So I was trying to find the ice, you know?" We nodded. "Well, I couldn't find it. I walked around the entire floor twice, and then I gave up, just trying to open every door. I knew it had to be around *somewhere*."

"You were just opening any door?" Natalie asked, incredulous.

"Well, every blank door. But they were all locked. But that's not the important part! Just wait!" He held his hand up like a stop sign, anxious to get to his point. "So I'm looking for ice, and then I open this one door, and it's not a room, it's a suite, and it's full of these Brazilian supermodels, and they thought I was room service, bringing them more bubble bath, but then I explained about the ice, and they saw the ice bucket, and then it turns out that they also needed ice, so then I went looking for it with this one guy from Wisconsin who was somehow part of their party, and we finally found it in this unmarked room near the elevator, and, anyway, they've got ice, and we've got ice," here he lifted up the now full ice bucket as if to prove his point, "but this guy's really cool, and he says we should come back and hang with all them."

He finally stopped and took a huge breath. We looked first at him and then each other.

"Did you say *Brazilian* supermodels?" Natalie asked.

Mark nodded enthusiastically. "So you wanna go?"

Natalie turned to me. "What do you think?"

"I dunno," I said slowly. "Seems like we should at least

95

check it out and see what it's like. If it's a weird scene, we can always come back here?"

I felt shy being put in the position of having to make any sort of decisive statement but also brave enough to keep pushing my own boundaries. Brazilian supermodels—*why not*? I scrutinized Natalie's face, trying to figure out what she was thinking.

She smiled, as if reading my mind. "You're right. Let's go check it out."

Getting out of the tub, she wrapped a towel around herself and tossed a second one to me. Just as we were about to put on our clothes, there was a knock at the door.

"Maybe that's the guy from Wisconsin!" Mark exclaimed, hurrying over toward the door.

He opened it, Natalie and I stepping slightly to the side, suddenly shy in our towels. It was not the mid-Western boy, though. It was room service. It was the ice cream Mark had ordered earlier in the evening. I guess he had told them the specific time he wanted it delivered, and then, in typical Mark fashion, forgotten about it completely. The room service delivery boy, however, seemed oblivious to our confusion and laughter, merely rolling the cart into the room, centering it in front of the bed, before turning to look at Mark expectantly.

"Oh. Right." Mark fumbled in his pockets, pulled out some bills, and gave them to the delivery boy.

As the door swung shut behind our messenger, Natalie and I stepped forward to investigate. The cart did, indeed, contain ice cream, but it "just" contained ice cream in the same way that a Ferrari is "just" a car. It was laid out in a way to make it as easy as possible to build your own sundae. There was a metal container with a lid, similar to an ice bucket, which contained scoops of what appeared to vanilla, strawberry, and chocolate ice cream. Another container featured several squares of soft and oozy brownies with nuts sprinkled across the top. As if that was not enough, there was another bowl of crumbled nuts and yet another container of

96

sliced bananas. To top it all off, there was a small crystal bowl of cherries and another bowl, complete with small spoons, of hot fudge.

Natalie and I looked at each other and laughed.

"You ordered this?" she asked Mark.

He laughed, coming over to have a look. "Yeah. I ordered it when we were still at the restaurant downstairs. I forgot about it. Looks good, doesn't it?"

He grinned at Natalie, who stuck her index finger in the hot fudge before bringing it to her lips for a slow lick.

"Mmmmm," she murmured, turning to me.

She stuck her index finger in the hot fudge again before bringing it to my lips. It was my turn to take a slow lick. It *was* delicious. Mark jutted his lower jaw forward, bringing his lips together in a pucker.

"My turn, my turn," he said, trying to be cute.

Natalie gave him a forced grin and shook her head. "Later."

He pouted, but she ignored him, still looking at me.

"I've got an idea," she said, with a low, breathy voice.

"What's that?" I asked.

"Do you trust me?"

I nodded. "I guess so."

"Good." She smiled, before turning to face Mark. "And I *know* you do."

He looked at her blankly before looking over at me, then back at her. He was clearly confused, which was about how I was feeling.

"I'm in charge now," she declared, "and I want you to lie on the bed."

Mark obediently lay down as she went into the bathroom. I could hear her rummaging for something, before coming out with two strips of narrow fabric.

"What's that?" I asked.

"Belts from the bathrobes."

She walked over to where Mark was stretched out and wrapped a belt around each of his wrists, tying each arm to

97

the headboard above him.

"What's going on?" he asked.

"You are going to feel everything," she said, "but you are not allowed to move or to watch."

"Aw, hun, how come?" he whined, while I did my best not to smirk.

I had no idea what we were going to do for which he had to be tied down, but all that mattered was that he was not allowed to touch me—and that Natalie and I would be together. The other stuff was not relevant.

By the time Natalie had finished tying him to the bed, she turned around and grinned at me.

"Ready?"

"Where do you want me?"

"You, my dear, are also on the bed. The towel, if you can, should be beneath Mark and most definitely *not* around you."

I could handle that. I shoved the towel under Mark (a little roughly, but he did not complain) before turning to face Natalie. Natalie briskly wheeled the ice cream cart beside the bed. She took one of the pieces of decorative fabric from the cart and draped it over Mark's eyes, tucking it under his head so that it would not slip off.

"Ready for dessert?" she asked me, cheerfully.

"I am!" Mark called out.

She looked over and gave him a withering glance that, unfortunately, he could not see, before turning back to face me with a beaming smile. She then clambered on the bed, so that we were each sitting on opposite sides of Mark's restricted body. It was clear that she was orchestrating all this, and orchestrating it well, so I willingly took a backseat in this operation, merely following her signals.

With the finesse of a porn star, she first moved her head back and forth, letting her hair brush against his stomach, his thighs, and his rapidly swelling cock. I knew that he could hear us breathing, but I also knew that he could not tell who was who, and that he would only get more confused as this

98

went on. I decided to mirror her behavior, running both my hair and my lips against his skin. I may not have been the biggest fan of Mark, but I could certainly enjoy tormenting him. His groans became gasps as she lightly ran her tongue over the edge of his cock, and I complied by licking his already swollen balls.

Natalie began to move her mouth up and down over his cock, her lips creating a firm grasp over his tight skin, my lips still caressing his balls and his inner thighs. We maintained our careful rhythm—fast enough to get him really riled up but not so fast that he would ruin her plans with an early orgasm. I had never felt this kind of power before, and I knew the effect it was having on me by the damp trails my pussy was leaving over the towel Natalie had thought to spread over the bed. I could also see and feel the effect it was having on Mark. I could only guess what it was doing to Natalie.

When his gasps and moans began to intensify, she stopped, and so I did the same, sitting up to see what she would to next. What she did next was reach over to the ice cream cart, take a scoop of vanilla ice cream, and let it fall directly on his chest. He inhaled suddenly, and I saw his wrists twitch, as though to move his arms before remembering that he could not. Triggered by the heat of his skin, the ice cream began to melt, running in white rivers across his chest. Natalie grinned, before bending over to lick it up, like a cat lapping up milk. That seemed like an excellent idea, and I followed.

The next scoop—strawberry this time—was deposited a bit lower down, more on his stomach than on his chest. Before I could lean over to start licking, Natalie held her hand up, as if to tell me to wait, while she retrieved a spoonful of hot fudge. With slow and careful precision, she maneuvered the full spoon over the bed until it was above the pink ice cream. Like a scientist working on a precarious experiment, she gradually angled the utensil so that the fudge trickled out, zig-zagging over the melting pink.

99

Mark inhaled again sharply, clearly surprised by the different temperature and sensation of this liquid, but Natalie ignored him as she bent over and ran her tongue across the blend of ice cream and hot fudge. I imitated, and it was delicious—not only the dessert, but also the view and proximity of Mark's swollen and otherwise ignored cock.

There were other spoonfuls, other combinations of hot fudge and nuts and cherries, which made their way across his body, leaving his formerly clean flesh littered with sticky remnants of sugar and saliva. We decorated his arms, we ate off his thighs, we kissed fudge off his balls and swallowed chocolate ice cream from his cock. We placed cherries on his nipples and nuts on his thighs, more ice cream on his stomach, and even more along the flesh just above his cock. We concealed the wrinkles of his balls with vanilla and the stretched pulsing of his cock with a combination of strawberry and vanilla.

All we did was lick and swallow. All he could do was squirm.

With a silent signal from Natalie, I knew we were done eating, and it was time for the next stage of the game. Her tongue wiped off his cock, while my mouth sucked his balls clean. We were killing him, and I almost felt sorry for him, but not enough to do anything about it yet. His wrists were tugging on the headboard, while his hips were gyrating up and down, desperately trying to get more of himself into our mouths.

"Mark?" she asked gently, lifting her head up off his cock.

"Mm-hm," was his feeble, sexually frustrated, response.

"Now it's time for you to participate. Are you ready?"

"Oh yes, yes," he gasped, straining at the wrist ties.

"Stop pulling," she commanded. "You're not done with those yet."

Natalie turned to face me and whispered into my ear, "Do you prefer penetration or tongue?"

I was not exactly sure where she was going with this,

100

but I answered honestly. "Penetration."

"Great." She grinned at me. "So you stay there."

Sitting up, she positioned herself so that her thighs were on either side of Mark's head, her pussy directly over his mouth.

"Now you've got to make me come before you get to come, got that?"

I think Mark said something, but it was impossible to tell through Natalie's body. I just saw her nod as she lowered herself an inch or two closer to his open lips. While I was struggling not to stare too obviously, she looked over her shoulder to see what I was doing. I, of course, was just staring like an idiot. She gestured to me with her hand to get on top of Mark. With a sigh of slippery satisfaction, I slid down over his cock, his massive swelling no match for the extraordinary wetness of my insides. Oh, it felt good.

I did not even try to pay attention to what the two of them were doing at the foot of the bed, so lost was I in the incredible sensation of this moment. In my own world, with my eyes closed, I just kept riding him, slow and even waves of pleasure coursing through my body. Whenever I felt like I wanted more, I just brought my index finger to my clitoris, rubbing circles over the growing nub, the dizzying sensation of internal pleasure coupling perfectly with the external sensation.

I had forgotten that we were supposed to be waiting for Natalie to come, so absorbed was in my own little rodeo. I was jolted back to the hotel room by her moans, by her body quivering above his head, her fingers gripping the headboard to stay upright. Riveted, I stopped moving, unable to stop watching. Seeing her come was hot, but hotter still was the realization that now it was all about Mark and me. Now I got to come.

Closing my eyes again, I kept rubbing my clit, shifting my hips back and forth against him, faster, faster, faster, until Mark cried out, his cock pulsating inside me, and I, too, came in a collapsed heap, all the more intense for the

101

prolonged foreplay that had preceded it.

You win! You got your ice-cream, and your iced cock, a double dessert.

You've had enough

With that aquatic orgasm, all my sexual tension and mid-twenties excuse for youthful energy drained out of me. I was exhausted. Suddenly the bathtub water felt a bit cold, and The Standard a bit dreary, and the huge overstuffed foot-shaped sculpture in the corner pretentious and ridiculous. It was time for me to leave. I had overstayed my welcome.

Leaving Mark and Natalie to cuddle sleepily and damply in the tub, I got out, grabbing one of the over-sized bathrobes to dry off.

"Where are you going?" Natalie murmured, not even turning her head.

"I gotta go," I said, pulling on my pants and searching for my bra.

Her head was still leaning against the edge of the tub, her eyes closed with the luxurious calm of the untroubled. Mark kept glancing over at me, but I could not tell the exact motivation for his surveillance, so I ignored him.

When I was ready to go, I leaned over the tub, giving first him a quick peck on the mouth, before giving her a slightly more intimate but still "on the way out" kind of kiss. They both seemed mildly concerned about the fact that I was leaving, but neither of them made any motion to get out of the tub, for which I was grateful. By this point, all I wanted was to get out of the hotel.

Luckily, my car was nearby, and it did not take long for me to get to Sunset Boulevard. Even though I could feel some of my earlier meal still lingering in my insides, I was not quite ready to go home yet, and I knew a greasy In-N-Out cheese sandwich would provide just the right amount of late night solace.

Turn to page 71.

103

Get him to leave

I held him close, listening to the pounding of his heart and feeling his breath. I figured I had to let him recover for a bit before I told him he had to go. We lay like that for several minutes, until both of us fell asleep, completely intertwined.

As usual, I woke up first. I just lay there, listening to the sound of his breathing, feeling the gentle twitches across the mattress as he shifted position. We had separated during the nap, as we often did, each of us preferring room to breathe while we slept, so I had a good vantage point from which to watch him. He looked so angelic when he slept, eyelashes fluttering slightly, mouth a tiny bit open. It was hard to believe that this was the boy who had stomped all over my heart less than a year ago. He was beautiful, but I knew how easily I could lose him again.

When he woke up, I smiled, his half-open eyes looking into mine.

"What time is it?" he muttered, spinning over onto his other side to look for his phone.

"I think we slept for about an hour," I replied coolly, swinging my legs over the edge of the bed as I sat up.

"What are you doing?" he asked.

"I'm going to take a quick shower," I told him, without turning around. "I've got dinner plans."

"Wait. Come back to bed."

I knew him well enough to time it perfectly. Just as he reached out to grab me, I stood up, and he missed me by inches.

"Oh, come back," he called out as I walked out of the room.

"Back in a minute," I said, before closing the bathroom door behind me.

104

Gripping the bathroom sink in my hands, I stared into the mirror, searching for power and self-control. Every piece of me wanted to run back into the room, to jump back into bed with him, but *no, no, no*. I gritted my teeth with determination. He would not make me do that. He did not have that kind of power. Before I could change my mind, and before he could come into the bathroom, I stepped into the shower and turned on the water.

Again, my timing was perfect. By the time it had occurred to him to come join me in the shower, I was innocently stepping out of it, towel wrapped demurely around my body.

"I was going to join you," he said, his voice trailing off with disappointment.

"Next time!" I told him cheerfully, with a peck on the cheek, as I headed back into my room to dress, leaving him looking a little lost and confused. "If you want a towel, you can use the one on the back of the door. Take your time, I just have to be out of here in twenty minutes."

"Where are you going?" His voice sounded so meek, it was almost embarrassing.

"Oh, I've got dinner plans," I repeated, again neglecting to add any more details.

Let him wonder, I thought. Let him wonder like I did all those nights. Let him know what it feels like to need someone who does not need you.

"Don't you want to take a shower together?" he asked again.

"Sorry, hon, I'm already dressed."

I breezed back into the bathroom in one of my nicer dresses, pretending I did not notice his obvious distress as I applied mascara and some sparkly eye shadow.

"I don't mean to rush you," I said, with the impersonal warmth of a receptionist, "but I do have to leave in about fifteen minutes, so if you want to take a shower..."

"Oh, that's okay, I'll just shower at home," he said, his body and tone both visibly crestfallen.

105

I did my best not to smile. I did my best not to notice, as I studied my face in the mirror and pulled my hair into a ponytail, how he was watching me. He returned to the bedroom to dress while I finished up in the bathroom. I was waiting for him to ask who my dinner plans were with, but I guess he knew better or did not want to hear the answer, because he never said anything more about it.

He got dressed quickly and then came out to join me in the living room. I could tell that he was disappointed that I had not come back into the room to catch the last glimpses of his nudity, but I did not have time for that. I was playing this game on a much larger scale.

"So, uh, I guess I should go now..." His voice trailed off as his shoulders gave the hint of a shrug.

Now I was trying to channel the perfect combination of complete friendly obliviousness.

"Sure, hon," I trilled, stepping over to the front door to give him a kiss goodbye.

I let him have one that was long enough to remind him of what we had just done in the bedroom, but also short enough that he knew nothing else would be happening between us without a little more work.

"If you have time after your dinner plans, you can call me..." Again, his voice trailed off. This time, like the last time, with more of a questioning tone than anything else.

"Sounds great!" I said. I would not, of course. I was going to make him miss me.

As I let the door close behind him, I exhaled slowly. I held onto the doorknob, knowing that it was all that stood between me and another kiss, and another, and another. I knew how much I wanted those kisses, and I knew how much he wanted to give them to me—now.

But if he was going to stick around, I had to make sure he appreciated me. He needed to want me the way I wanted him. I had done the right thing for tonight. Now let him squirm!

106

You win. Feels good, doesn't it?

Keep hanging out

I held him close, listening to the pounding of his heart and feeling his breath. We lay like that for several minutes, until both of us fell asleep, completely intertwined.

It was wonderful waking up beside him. As usual, I woke up first, and I just listened to the sound of his breathing, feeling the gentle twitches across the mattress as he shifted position. We had separated during the nap, as we often did, each of us preferring room to breathe while we slept, so I had a good vantage point from which to watch him. He looked so angelic when he was asleep, the eyelashes fluttering slightly, the mouth a tiny bit open. It took all my self-control not to touch him but just to stare at him from across the distance of my pillow. He was beautiful.

When he woke up, I smiled, his half-open eyes looking into mine.

"What time is it?" he muttered, spinning over onto his other side to look for his phone.

"I think we slept for about an hour," I murmured lovingly, slithering across the bed toward him.

I draped my left arm across his chest, curving my body against his back. He stiffened, shaking my arm off as he turned around.

"What are you doing?" he asked.

"What am I doing?" I stared at him, confused. "I just wanted to hold you."

"I told you, I don't like cuddling in bed. It makes me feel claustrophobic." He shook his body slightly as if shaking off a spider.

I knew for a fact that that was not true. Throughout the course of our relationship, we had always held each other in bed. It only started being problematic near the end.

"Darling, I'm sorry, I just thought things might be

108

different now…?"

"Different now, why? Because we had sex? Nothing's changed. I'm still me, and you're still you, and we're not going to work together—this time or any other time."

He got out of bed and began putting on his clothes. I blinked. It was as though he was a different person now that he had gotten off. I wished desperately that I could move time backwards, try something else, say something else, anything, whatever. I wished all this at the same time that I knew I had done nothing wrong, other than, of course, having sex with him too quickly. Maybe if I had made him wait, maybe if I had made him fall in love with me first, maybe if I had just…

You lose. Better luck next time!

109

Go home

Maybe if it had not been so late, I would not have been averse to getting messy, but this just seemed like a cheap alternative to playing with knives, and I preferred to be more rested when cutting my heart up into pieces. So I bid my hot bartender a short goodbye (to her credit, she did ask if I was "alright," but what does one say to that, really, but "of course"?) before making my way out to my car. I could not pretend that I was not sad, but I knew that, for once, I was making a sensible judgment call, and I knew I would be happy I had done so in the morning.

Los Angeles was a great place in which to drive—at night—and I gloried in the empty streets and quick stoplights. I even took the freeway for one exit, just for the thrill of the easy merge. By the time I had gotten home, I had managed to cheer myself up. I decided to make myself some late night pasta before heading to bed.

My roommate was sound asleep, so I had the apartment to myself as I bustled around the kitchen. I put some water on to boil, chopped up some garlic and onions to add to the marinara sauce already in the fridge, and pulled out some cheese to sprinkle on top once everything was done. The water was rattling around the edges of the lid by this point, so I added my favorite wheat-free pasta, turned the fire off under the bubbling sauce, and turned to look around me. I had planned to tidy the kitchen while I waited for the noodles to cook, but my roommate had actually left everything in pretty good shape, so there was not really anything to do.

Leaning with my back against the sink, I stared at the yellow pot that was holding my cooking pasta. I watched the steam curling out around the edges of the lid. A watched pot may not boil, but this pot was already boiling, so there

110

seemed to be no harm in staring, plus there was something vaguely hypnotic about watching the steam and listening to the water gurgling. As I stared, I realized that my clothes had suddenly gotten uncomfortable. I had been wearing these same clothes for almost twelve hours now. My jeans felt stiff and claustrophobic, so I quickly tugged them off, tossing them over one of the dining room chairs.

Since my roommate was asleep, I did not think twice about tossing my bra on top of the pants. Even if she had been awake, it would not have been an issue, since she and I often walked around the apartment half-naked, but, since she was asleep, it definitely was not an issue. It felt good to be unencumbered by confining clothes, and now the steam was even more hypnotic. Before I even realized what I was doing, my fingers were drifting between my legs.

With the kitchen sink pressing into my spine, with nothing more erotic in front of me than boiling pasta on a stove, my fingers seemed drawn on their own accord to my freshly accessible underwear. I was so tired, it did not take much to make me zone out, tilt my head back, close my eyes, and let my fingers do their work.

I started off with a few circles around my clitoris, enjoying the sensation of blood racing there, feeling the swelling against my fingertip, before I began alternating slipping the same finger inside me and then moving it back to my clitoris. When I did not have any lube on hand, this was my usual procedure, smearing the gathering wetness of my insides over my clit, enjoying the teasing essence of continuous finger movement. I was usually too lazy to masturbate with my finger, but tonight I was too lazy to head back to the bedroom. Plus I had to keep an eye on the pasta!

So I stayed in the kitchen, panties shoved to one side, hand running on batteries of its own, circle-circle-circle, inside, then outside, inside, then outside, back-and-forth and back-and-forth. Repeat. I tried to coax a fantasy out of my brain, but it was too tired, too half-distracted by the food cooking on the stove, to be properly cooperative. Instead, I

111

got more of an MTV-style montage, flashes of recent bodies I had touched and that had touched me. I thought of Natalie, I thought of my ex, I thought of her breasts and his cock, of the way she had kissed me and the way he had fucked me, of the look on her face when I took off my clothes, of the look on his face when his cock slid inside me.

My nipples were hardening, and I slipped my left hand under my shirt to tug gently on my left breast. I could feel him doing that, feel him flicking his tongue over both nipples in succession, and I moaned quietly as the edge of the counter nudged into my back. I glanced over at the pasta pot. It was definitely ready to be emptied, but that would have to wait. I turned the fire off and turned my attention back to myself. This had to get finished.

I turned the light off in the kitchen, letting the dim glow of the parking garage neon blend with the early morning sun across my skin. With a smile, I pressed one hand back between my legs, while the other went back to tugging on my now quite hard nipples. My eyes closed, I could see him standing in front of me, could feel her breath on my neck. The kitchen disappeared, the kitchen sink no longer pressing into my back. There were no spatial elements in the darkness of my head, just two people, with their bodies against mine.

I tilted my hips so that my right hand could slide in a bit deeper when it pushed its way inside, and spread my legs, so that my clitoris was even more available, the cool night air a pleasing contrast to the heat radiating from my insides. Circle-circle-circle, inside, then outside, inside, then outside, back-and-forth and back-and-forth. Repeat. Faster. Deeper. Round and round, until it was no longer necessary to slide inside, when there was so much slippery wetness all over everything that I did not need anymore, and then it just came down to my clitoris, and the circles. Again and again with the circles, my fatigue completely drowned out by my desire until it all came with a rush, starting with a flicker of potential that became a wave of sensation, and I slid down the kitchen cabinet until I was sitting on the floor, quivering

112

with pleasure, a sweaty smile on my face.
It was now time to eat.

You win. Bon appetit.

A little more trouble

I was already there, I did not feel like driving home in the depressing early hours of the morning, and maybe, I thought, trying to convince myself, I should not be so quick to judge other's behavioral practices. With all this running through my mind, I took the hand that was being offered to me and followed Natalie into the bedroom.

Getting into bed first, allotted the right side against the wall, I watched her as she finalized her before-bed preparations. She really was beautiful, and in the soft light raking through the blinds, she looked like a cross between Angelina Jolie and Jean Seberg. With relatively little self-consciousness, I studied the curve of her ass, the line of the arch at the end of her endless legs, the perfect roundness of her hips. Even the precision of her collarbone seemed designed by a craftsman, and it was with the feeling of a child on Christmas morning that I wrapped my arms around her as she got into bed.

Although I had not expected to get much sleep, I passed out moments after she did, the sound of her dog's breathing from the base of the bed somehow comforting, the feeling of her body against mine clearly less distracting after being awake for so many hours. I had told myself I would not sleep, that I would just feel her for the hours I had allotted, but that conviction did not last, and before I realized it, she was stroking my arm.

"Buon giorno," she whispered, presenting me with a tiny glass of black Italian espresso.

I smiled at the exotic nature of the moment, taking the glass from her and swallowing its contents with three small mouthfuls. She smiled at me for an instant, taking the empty container and placing it on the bedside table.

"When did you get up?" I asked, startled that I had not

114

woken up when she got out of bed, much less when she got dressed.

"About half an hour ago," she murmured to my neck, snuggling up against me, her sweatshirt and shorts soft and cool against my skin. "I just went and walked Akira and made some coffee."

"I'm sorry I slept through that."

She made a small snorting laugh that tickled against my skin. "You didn't miss anything, and I came back to bed as soon as I could..."

I turned to face her. I thought fleetingly that I should brush my teeth and check my smudged makeup, but she kissed me, so I could not have been that bad. I remembered how exquisite a woman's body could be, how incredibly smooth and gentle—the joints, the bones, the flesh more delicate than any boy's. I grabbed her tightly, loving the feeling of her lips against mine, no trace of morning stubble to scratch my face, even the teeth somehow more perfect. This girl was damn beautiful. I had wanted to touch every part of her. I did not want to let go. Even though I happily dated men, and sadly tried to recover from the loss of my ex through dating more men, I knew that my impressions of them were never as vivid as my impressions of women. I never felt quite like devouring a man I adored in the way I wanted to devour this woman.

Men were always a scattershot of moments, pieces, and, while this girl was also a cacophony of beautiful parts, these parts fused together into a glowing whole. At the same time, I knew this was a girl I would never be able to hold onto. I knew she belonged to someone else, and I was not interested in competing for priority status—or even in settling for equal status. I was not that progressive. I would just grab the time I had this morning, and that would be that.

I started to slip my fingers between her legs, searching for the warm wetness I knew I would find, but she slid back, out of reach.

"I want to do you, if that's okay," she purred in my ear,

115

my hand drifting useless over the bed, somewhere between her body and mine.

"Okay, sure."

What else could I say? I rolled over on my back, hands out to my side, hip-level, legs spread. I felt vaguely like I was preparing for an autopsy, and even Natalie laughed at my readiness.

"Have you ever done it with two?" she asked.

"With two…what?" I lifted my head up, straining to see what she was doing. She was rummaging in one of the drawers of her dresser.

"Two vibrators," she answered, turning to face me with one in either hand.

One was a normal size, two double A batteries big, and covered with a bright floral pattern. The other was the equivalent length of my pinky finger but thicker, like a longer version of my thumb. It was a solid navy blue.

"No. No, I can't say that I've ever done it with two."

"Great. So get ready for me to blow your mind," she exclaimed, jumping back on the bed and reaching into the bedside table for a tube of KY jelly. "I'd never have thought to do it with two, or even to look twice at something so small," here she gestured toward me with the more diminutive vibrator as she carefully applied lube to the tips of both, "but I got this one at a Babeland workshop I went to, and I tried it out one day when I was bored, and, well," she turned to look at me, grinning, "it was pretty fucking rad."

I grinned back. "Bring it on. I can't wait."

Lying back down, I resumed my derivation of corpse pose, keeping myself pliable, so she could adjust me. She bent my knees slightly, which spread me open a bit more, and then she curled up beside me. The small vibrator was inserted into my pussy while the big vibrator trained on my clitoris. It *was* pretty fucking rad, she was right. I closed my eyes to lose myself fully.

The smaller vibrator just moved in and out in little increments, while the primary focus of the sensation was on

116

the outer and inner rims, which started to feel like the central focus of my entire being. The larger vibrator just kept moving in unrelenting circles around my clitoris, sometimes a little more to the left, sometimes a little more to the right, but always consistently *there*. Occasionally, the vibrators would veer a little, not quite converging, but close enough that the waves of vibration would coincide, and then I would grip the sheet in my hand as my eyes rolled back in my head, my chest rising with the deep inhale. Then she would veer the vibrators apart again, the smaller one going further in, the larger one drawing circles further up, and I would collapse with my exhales.

It went on like this, on and on, converging, coinciding, veering, circling, and collapsing, until everything seemed to quicken, the movements growing more intense, the waves rushing over my whole body rather than feeling localized, and I started to quiver, in my pussy at first, around my clitoris, but then, as I gripped the sheets harder, the quivering spread to my toes, my legs, my arms, until then, with a huge moan, everything exhaled, everything collapsed, and I lay, shivering, on the bed, at the mercy of every wave of sensation running through me.

Natalie switched the vibrators off, placing them on the floor before turning to wrap herself around me. We lay in silence for a moment before I could muster a thank you, to which she kissed me on the shoulder in response. We lay in silence a bit longer.

"Want to go for a drive?" she asked me suddenly, rolling over onto her stomach, staring me straight in the eyes.

I looked at her and laughed. She seemed to have no interest in me returning the favor, so in lieu of that, I would certainly follow her wherever she wished to go

"A drive? Sure. Where?"

"I don't know." She gestured toward the windows. "It's a beautiful day. We can put the top down, take Akira to the beach or a park or something. Have a picnic."

117

I smiled. "Oh yeah, I forgot you had a convertible."

She grinned back. "Yup. Let's use that shit."

Natalie bounded out of the bed. I watched her long, lean body as she pulled on a teeny tiny pair of lace underwear, skinny boot cut jeans, a red bra, and started buttoning a black Oxford-style shirt. It was not that I had forgotten about her boyfriend of refrigerator-photo fame, it was that I was choosing not to think about it. I was choosing to think, instead, of the fact that I was going driving with this exceptionally hot lady, and that, whatever we did, wherever we were headed, he would not be there.

"Come on, lady. Get up." Laughing, she mock-kicked me, before tugging the blankets off my body. "Look at that. Naked girl in my bed."

Beaming back at her, I spread my legs seductively. "Are you sure you want to get up...?" I asked, with a seductive pout.

"Tease!" she scolded me. "I want to get up—with you. I want to take a drive—with you. Of course," she leaned over pensively, her face inches from mine, "getting dressed is optional, but considering the state of dog hair on car seats, I'd recommend at least underwear!"

With a final peck on the lips for emphasis, she darted out of the room. "Just gonna clean up the car a bit. Back in a sec!"

I laughed as I hauled myself out of bed. My clothes were still on the floor where I had thrown them, and it did not take more than a minute to pull them back on. Wandering out of her room, I steadfastly avoided the kitchen with the perturbing photograph, opting instead to hover in the living room, scanning her rows of CDs and DVDs, while I waited for the clomp-clomp of her shoes as she and Akira made their way back to the apartment.

She was right. It did not take them long.

"Look at that, you're up and ready!" she proclaimed as they whisked into the house, Akira heading straight for the water bowl.

"That I am," I said, as she stepped up close to me, hips to hips, breasts to breasts, lips to lips.

She gave me one long hungry kiss before pulling back. "I gotta brush my teeth!" she exclaimed, "And then let's go!"

Natalie took her turn in the bathroom while I stood around awkwardly, and then it was my turn to use her guest toothbrush. I stared at my face in the mirror. I definitely looked like I was ready for the walk of shame. Last night's makeup was crusted beneath my eyes, my hair screamed sex, and I looked sleepy, but no matter. This was all part of the experience.

I scraped off the makeup with some of Natalie's products, gave myself a good wash, borrowed her brush, and made myself moderately presentable. It did not take long, and I felt a million times more human.

By the time I stepped out of the bathroom, Natalie had filled a brown paper Trader Joe's bag with some bottled water, a loaf of wheat-free bread, a slab of cheese, some edamame, olives, and a bag of grapes. Not bad for a last minute scramble. I smiled at her, leaning over for another kiss. This one was sweet and minty-fresh.

"Yum," she said with a grin. "Let's get this show on the road."

"Can I carry anything?"

She looked around the kitchen but just shook her head. "I think I've got it all here. You can carry Akira's leash, if you like."

I grabbed the purple plastic retractable leash from the table near the door. Akira bounded over toward us, leading the way down the stairs to the street. There it was, the cute sporty red convertible, parked just in front of my comparably dingy car. Natalie opened up the driver's side door, letting Akira jump in before sticking the bag of food in the trunk.

"Hop in!" she told me, as she slid behind the steering wheel.

I got in the car, feeling like I was from another

119

generation as I marveled at the automatically receding top. The surprisingly consistent Los Angeles sun poked its way through the growing crack, spreading its uncompromising brilliance over the car. Akira seemed buoyant as always, bounding back and forth from one side of the car to the other.

"Do you have sunglasses?" Natalie asked, watching me wince.

I shook my head. For various reasons, I had not thought to bring them when I went out last night. "Oh, wait," I said, remembering. "I've got an extra pair in my glove compartment."

When I got back from my car, the extra pair protectively on my face, she handed me a baseball cap. I noticed that she had also put one on.

"Take it, you'll be glad you did."

I happily slipped some L.A. Dodgers support on my head, feeling instantly more comfortable within my cocoon of shade.

"Fabulous!" she declared. "Let's hit the road!"

Hypnotized by the pattern of light on the road and the wind on my face, the rhythmic pattern of Akira's panting and the distraction of her frequent hand on my thigh, I did not even pay attention to the route, to the freeways we got on and off, to the surface streets with their twinkling stoplights and click-click turn signals, until suddenly we were parking, and Natalie was tugging me with one hand and Akira was tugging her other. We were traipsing and laughing through the woods, down a path, up a hill, and then over a pass, until there was a beautiful, quiet clearing, a picturesque pond in front of us, trees all around vigilantly maintaining our privacy.

"Where are we?" I asked in wonder.

"My secret place," she said, grinning, as she shook the blanket straight over the ground.

While I stood still, confused and amazed, staring at the nature surrounding us, marveling that we were somewhere in (or at least near) Los Angeles, Natalie sat down on the blanket, released Akira from the leash to sniff the surrounding grass, positioned the food and drinks, and slipped her top over her head.

I looked down at her. She smiled at me.

"Will you rub some lotion on my back?" she asked.

"No problem," I said, bending down behind her.

I took the sunscreen from her extended hand and squirted a dollop on her exposed skin. What I was doing would have been erotic even if she had worn a bathing suit, but knowing that she was naked from the waist up, while the slippery goo ran down her back, around her sides, glistening over her skin and making her breasts bright, was even more stimulating than I could ever have imagined. There was something tender about what I was doing, something warm and vaguely maternal, that seemed to give it another dimension of sensuality.

"Are you going to take your pants off?" I asked.

"You want me to?" She looked at me over her shoulder, a teasing expression on her face.

"Well, you know...if you're going to take them off, I should get you there with the sunscreen, too."

With a smile, she slipped her jeans off, tossing them to the side. I used that as my cue to start with her toes, slowly making my way up her legs to her thighs, waist, and then arms. I went up the left leg first, before making my way back down to her right toes. Tantalizingly slow as I caressed her inner thighs, I pretended not to notice the darkening stain on her lace underwear. I could feel the same kind of stain forming between my legs, but I kept feigning obliviousness.

We had not eaten any food yet today, so I left a lubed up Natalie lying on her stomach to examine the contents of the bag.

"Do you want something to eat?" I asked.

"Yes," she replied, turning to face me. "You."

I grinned back at her, handing her a piece of bread and a slice of cheese. She munched on the bread, which looked

121

tempting enough—especially entering her lips—for me to help myself to a piece. We ate in silence for a minute, finishing our slices, before she brushed the crumbs off her fingers.

"Want me to do you?" she asked.

I blinked. She laughed.

"With sunscreen, silly. The other stuff will happen later!"

I tugged my shirt off, and Natalie gave me the same sort of application I had given her—slow and thorough, beginning at the neck, working down the shoulders, across the lower back, lingering over the ass, and finishing with my toes. Just when I thought I was relaxed enough to fall asleep, she started making her way back up. There was no way I could fall asleep with those hands anywhere near my inner thighs. I did my best not to squirm as she reached closer to treacherous territory, and I willed myself to stop leaking through my underwear. I was so turned on by her fingers that my clitoris was beginning to throb.

"You know what I brought?" Natalie whispered in my ear.

"What's that?" I asked, rolling halfway around so that I could face her.

In response, she merely stood up and went over to her bag. She rummaged through it for a moment, retrieving a small bottle.

"What's that?" I asked again, squinting in an attempt to make it out.

She came closer to me, kneeling with one leg on either side of my waist. She held the bottle right near my face.

"It's chocolate body syrup," she said, with satisfaction. "For dessert!"

I smiled, but more at her pleasure than out of a personal excitement for what she had planned, as I still did not completely understand what she had in mind.

"Turn over," Natalie commanded.

I did as I was told.

122

Her legs were still on either side of my waist, knees on the ground, my upper torso exposed for her consumption. With a devilish grin, she dramatically uncapped the bottle and tossed the lid to one side. With a look of utmost seriousness on her face, she removed what appeared to be a small brush-like implement from the side of the bottle, carefully wiggled it around inside the bottle, and then extracted it with a flourish. Like a painter, she whisked the brush around my chest, drawing squiggly lines and circles with the mastery of an Abstract Expressionist. More feminine than Pollock, these lines tenderly traced my curves, ran rings around my breasts, and left dollops on my nipples.

There was something pleasing about the childlike sensuality of her actions. I lay back, relaxed, turned-on, entertained as she became fully immersed in her work. My eyes were closed when I realized that she had paused. I opened them to see her watching me.

"You're not falling asleep, are you?"

I shook my head. "No way. Not possible. I'm enjoying this a *lot*."

She grinned again. "Good. Now time for part two. Cleaning you up!"

Carefully capping the bottle, she placed it to the side. She positioned her knees properly and then leaned over. She started by licking the chocolate off my right nipple and then my left. I moaned. It felt amazing. It must have been pretty obvious to Natalie that any attention paid to my nipples made me squirm with delight and frustration. Having licked both of them clean, she kept a firm, twisting grip on the right one while her attention turned to the rest of my torso.

Squirming was an understatement. As her tongue made its deliberate journey over the rings and squiggles, cutting straight lines and curving over circular ones, the consistent tug on my right nipple made me feel like not only my entire pussy, but my entire *body*, was wide open, aching to be touched and caressed. She obviously read my mind, or at least noticed the desperate twisting and shifting of my body,

123

because suddenly her hands were cupped underneath my ass, squeezing it, and her tongue was between my thighs. I knew there was no chocolate there, but she licked it clean, just the same, interspersed with teasing darts across my clitoris.

I was aching, but I refused to beg. Luckily, Natalie seemed to have the same goals I did. The flicking grew more frequent, the darts longer, and, before a minute had passed, her face was completely against my pussy, her tongue licking my clitoris with as much determination as she had used to clean my chest, her index finger circling just inside my entrance.

By this point, I was gripping the ends of the picnic blanket in my hands, oblivious to the sky above or the potential of being seen. I could not hear anything, and I certainly was not looking around. My entire universe was focused between my legs.

I could feel myself clenching, the muscles in my pussy tightening and releasing, tightening and releasing, as blood pulsed everywhere. My clitoris felt large and swollen, and I could tell that I was dripping wet. My eyes were closed; there was nothing that I needed to see. Her index finger gradually slid further inside, quarter inch by quarter inch, pulling out, pushing in, every time a little bit further, the tongue always loving, always there.

Gripping the blanket was not doing me any good. When the time came, I came, and my entire body seized up, minor convulsions across my inner thighs, toes clenched like a neurotic ballerina, upper body twisting left then right, hips grounding into the grass, while she fucked me with one last thrust of finger and tongue, body arching upwards, out of my control, like a marionette commanded by the minute motions of her finger, until I collapsed, breathing heavily, and she fell down beside me, hand clutching mine, both of us gazing upwards, clouds mocking us with their calm and easy serenity while our chests heaved, and sweat cooled across our temples.

You win. Your forecast is for sunny skies and complicated women.

Try your luck

I was not sure I would know what to do with Natalie and Mark alone, but I certainly did not feel comfortable heading off with a group of people I had only just met, and, well, Natalie and I did have a history of sorts, so maybe it would not be too weird—or so I kept reminding myself as I followed them out into the parking lot.

All three of us had separate cars, so Natalie rode with Mark, leaving her car behind in the parking lot, while I followed them to Mark's place. Mark lived downtown, just off Main Street at 7th, in one of those renovated loft buildings that used to be warehouses or factories or something and was now fancy new apartments for the bourgeoisie.

When I first got to L.A., I had briefly considered moving into one myself, seduced by the pool-on-the-roof concept and the included gym, but then I realized that I was not bourgeois enough to afford the rent (shockingly high considering the presence of crack addicts and lack of supermarkets in the surrounding streets), plus, after clocking time in New York City, I had developed a proclivity for trees in my older age, of which downtown offered few. So I did not end up living there, but I loved to visit, and I certainly loved to use the pools.

Mark obviously could afford living alone, so his loft was not awkwardly segmented by screens or strategically placed bookcases, sprawling, instead, in cement-like sparseness in all directions. A tidy bedroom had been improvised in one corner, complete with black sheets and bedspread, an expensive Ikea-lookalike lamp, and a tiny wood bedside table. The other corner was apparently the living room, and it featured a white leather couch, a flat screen television marking the division of the space, a larger

126

version of the same lamp from the bedroom, and a glass coffee table. The kitchen was just a wall of stainless steel.

I took it all in with rapid envy before turning to Natalie and Mark. They were talking under their breath while removing coats and bags, stashing theirs and mine in a closet beside the door. I felt awkward. I did not know how to treat the silence, if it was my job to avoid it or theirs. Shoving my hands into my pockets, I stood there for a moment, watching them, before doing the verbal equivalent of clearing my throat.

"What do you guys feel like doing?"

They turned to stare at me, and I felt like a clod. Was I in junior high? Who says that? Who says that in situations like this? Who, actually, ends up in situations like these? Who *was* I? I wanted to grab my coat and leave. Everything about this moment was awkward—until Natalie smiled at me, and then I remembered how much I wanted to fuck her.

She walked over to me, her eyes staring straight at mine.

"Can I get you something to drink?"

For some reason, those words seemed to be asking something else entirely, only I was not sure what. Was she asking me to take my clothes off? There was a subtext to this whole dynamic that my social translator was not picking up. Rather than answer her question with a response that might be incorrect or inadequate, I replied with a question of my own.

"Does your building have a pool?" I asked, turning to Mark, who was still standing by the door.

He smiled. "We've got a pool *and* a hot tub. They close at ten, but it's really easy to jump the fence." A pause. A glance at Natalie. A glance back at me. "Want to use them?"

At least I knew what happened in a pool. Although, on second thought, I had no idea what Mark and Natalie would want to do in a pool, but at least we would be *in* a pool, which was already a good idea. I nodded and grinned back at him.

127

"Perfect! Sounds great. Want to grab some towels, Nat?"

"Sure."

She ducked into the bathroom, emerging with three very fluffy matching white towels, not at all the kind of towel I would expect a boy to own. I wondered how much time Natalie spent in this apartment, or if Mark was one of those boys who bought things like that as a way of appearing grown up and sophisticated.

"Should I carry anything?" I asked.

"I don't think we need anything else," Mark replied, looking at Natalie. She shook her head. "Alright then, let's go!"

Grabbing his keys, Mark led the way out of the apartment, locking the door behind him. I followed him and Natalie down the hall. He lived so close to the top of the building that we did not even have to get back in the elevator. There was a special stairwell just to the left of the elevator marked "Pool," and up that flight of stairs we went, through a heavy door an official fire department sign sternly told us not to prop, and then we were out on the roof.

It was an amazing night, totally silent this high up from the street, dawn curling up around the edges, the downtown landscape stretching out around us. This part of the city always amazed me, feeling so much less like a Los Angeles that I usually experienced.

Natalie and Mark climbed over the gate, dropping the towels on the ground ahead of them. Natalie turned to give me a hand over, which I told her I did not need. The gate was barely three feet high, using its boldly printed hours of operation as more of a deterrence than actual physical heft. It would be opening again in several hours, I noted, but for now I hoisted myself over, happy that we were not sharing the pool with anyone else.

Natalie placed the towels on one of the chairs near the pool, and then, staring straight at me, yanked her shirt over her head, placing it neatly by the stack of white fluffy

128

towels. With a hint of a smile and a wink, she slid out of her pants, tossing them on the back of the same chair. It only took a few more seconds until her bra and panties were draped in the same place.

With a squeal, she did a cannonball-esque jump into the water, sending spray in both my and Mark's directions. Mark laughed and tugged his shirt off, throwing it and his jeans over the towels without even looking. His jeans fell on the floor, but I was the only one who noticed. They were already making out in the pool.

Realizing that I was more awkward outside the water than in, I quickly slipped out of my clothes, placing them on a different chair, and then, while I stood hesitantly at the edge of the pool, Natalie pulled away from Mark to call out to me.

"Come on, lady. Get in already!"

"It feels great," Mark added, doing some kind of doggie-style splash around Natalie.

As I said, more awkward outside than in, and especially so naked, which left me with little choice but to comply. I took the stairs, though (cannonballs had never been my speed), walking down the three that led into the shallow end of the pool. Like many of the on-the-rooftop style, it was a perfect rectangle of carefully heated blue, and it did feel great.

I could not remember the last time I had gone swimming naked, and quite possibly never had, but I instantly wished I had had more opportunities in which to do so. More than great, it felt *amazing*. The water caressed my skin, my breasts, running between my legs. It was like rolling around between incredibly expensive silk sheets that somehow managed to be everywhere at once. I twirled, like an underwater ballerina, stretching my legs and arms around me, until, suddenly, Natalie was behind me, embracing me, licking my throat, hands covering my breasts.

I was now completely awake, jolted out of whatever reverie the late night and water had lulled me into moments

129

before. It was an odd sensation, all my nerves suddenly electric, especially my clitoris, which pulsed as water flowed in and out of it. I tilted my head back, falling against Natalie, letting my feet come off the floor of the pool. I wrapped my arms around her, my hands clutching her ass, which was tight and smooth in my hands.

Natalie started to pinch my nipples, and I fell in love with the sensation of such pleasure mixed with the feeling of underwater weightlessness. I had forgotten about him for a minute, but then there was Mark, standing in front of me, his arms actually around Natalie, which left me somewhere in between, his mouth on mine, his cock conspicuous between my legs. He alternated between pressing his tongue deeply into my mouth and gently biting my lips.

I felt almost confused, caught in the crossfire of his energy against my front and Natalie's against my back, all of us surrounded, womb-like, by the water. I could hear blood pounding in my ears, overshadowing any sound of waves or breathing.I moaned as Mark started to press his way into me, Natalie intensifying the pressure on my nipples, and then he grabbed my hips, slippery inside the pool, and shoved his cock into me with one emphatic motion. I did not know if to scream or moan, so I did a combination of both, silenced by Mark's mouth over mine. Arching my back, Natalie and Mark wrapped themselves around me even more tightly, and we were so close that it was almost like Mark was fucking both of us.

There was no way to support myself, no way to brace myself against the force of his thrusting, no way, in fact, to do much of anything but succumb. If they had not been there, on either side of me, I would have literally floated away. But with this set-up? Quite the opposite. I was grounded, without much choice of movement, while Natalie kept kissing my neck, Mark kept kissing my mouth, and everything was a blur of pleasure and sensation and depth and force. We were all wet, even the parts of our bodies above the water.

130

I thought I had felt it all, until Natalie slid one of her hands between my body and Mark's, somehow managing to get her fingers between my legs and over my swollen clit. With Mark still kissing me passionately, there was no way for me to look around to see what was going on. I could only feel, and I felt her circular pressure in waves of electric currents running through my body. I could feel my orgasm building, and I knew Mark's was coming soon, too, his thrusting picking up speed, as he stopped kissing me, merely breathing quicker and quicker over my damp face.

With his mouth off mine, I could hear my moans now, as well, and they were getting louder, feeling foreign to a normally vocally reserved me.

"Keep going," I gasped, hoping that Natalie would know I was referring to her.

Either way, neither Natalie nor Mark stopped, both of them picking up speed and force in a way that made me feel like I would split in two.

I came, crying out, with a voice that did not sound like mine, while Mark, clearly turned on by my orgasm, shoved in three more rapid times until, with one last push, he came, shooting white cum into the water of the pool. I came again, or maybe I was still coming, the waves of sensation mirroring the waves of the pool, falling back into Natalie, who wrapped her arms around me, everything rippling in all directions.The two of us stayed like that, Mark drifting slightly away, as we all struggled to catch our breath. When I looked up, he was leaning against the far edge of the pool, elbows up on the ledge, grinning at both of us. I slipped out of Natalie's grip, turning to look at her. She smiled at me, her face and hair both wet.

With a look over at Mark, I said to her, "But which one of us is going to take care of you?"

She smiled at me. "I was rather hoping you would."

I smiled back. "Under the water or above?"

"Oh, let's stay in the pool," she exclaimed. "It's far too cold to get out now!"

131

With a confidence that could only have come post-orgasm, I pushed her thighs apart with my hand. Staring straight at her, I slipped my hand between her legs, watching her eyes close as she tilted her head back, leaning her body against the edge of the pool. Rubbing small circles around her clitoris, I was rewarded with a moan that encouraged me to pick up speed and pressure, and also to lean down, covering her nipple with my tongue and teeth.

I tried to pay attention to the signs she was giving me, using them to know when and where to alternate pressure, feeling her breathing become short and accelerated, watching the way she gripped the pool with her hands, arms spread out, Jesus-like against the morning sky. Taking a big gulp of air, I slid underwater, placing my head between her legs. I wanted to feel her, underwater. I had swum in high school and college and could hold my breath for a fairly long time. I doubted she had done this before, and, even if she had, I could feel and hear her moans of vigorous enthusiasm from my position. That was all the validation I needed.

Exploring her pussy as best I could, while she grabbed at my shoulders, I moved my tongue in sloppy loops around her clitoris, clockwise circles of pressure, until I could not do it any more. I quickly stood up, took another swallow of air, before heading back down. It did not take long, especially not after I slipped one finger inside her wet pussy, leaving it there even when I reached up for more air.

"You're amazing," she gasped, as I headed down for the third time.I could hear her moaning get louder even through the water, and she began to grab my shoulders with even more aggression. I shoved my tongue and fingers harder, knowing I was running out of air but desperate to finish. Suddenly, she stiffened, and then, with an "Oh my god" that I was sure echoed around downtown, she sagged against me, and I came up to the surface for the last time, taking in one well-deserved breath of air.

She wrapped her arms around me like a child who has forgotten how to swim, and I held her like that, the two of us

132

floating against the edge of the pool. I glanced over my shoulder to see where Mark had gone. He was still in the same place, elbows propped up on the far end of the pool, grinning at us. I smiled back and then turned away. I was over him. There was something far more intimate about the sound of Natalie's heartbeat against my chest, her damp hair tracing tendrils along my shoulders.

The moment was broken, of course, as the third party in our equation wanted to get involved. Mark swam over to us with a noisy splashing that seemed brutal to my ears, and then, with a "Hey, ladies" that made me cringe, threw his arms around the two of us. We were a trio of love. I tried not to roll my eyes.

"That was great," he said, breathing heavy in my ear.

Suddenly, I felt that post-orgasmic weirdness, when hormones have settled and vision becomes clear. His affections felt lecherous, full of the creepiness of the voyeur, and I wished that he would disappear so I could swim with Natalie, alone. I knew the two of them were a package deal, so I was torn between this smarmy mess or reconciling my weirdness with him so that I could keep hanging out with her.

What do you do?

Escape the smarminess?
(turn to page 153)
or
Stick around and see what happens next?
(turn to page 170)

He should make the first move

I figured I had had enough shameless behaviour for one night, so I played it demure. Unfortunately, he played it predictably professional, so too quickly I was on my way home alone, cheese sandwich in a bag on the seat beside me, without any sort of romantic exchange, no sparkly dialogue, and, most sadly, no plans to meet again later. I consoled myself with the fact that at least he worked near my house, and I was very fond of cheese sandwiches, so maybe the future would provide another opportunity.

You lose. Better luck next time!

Try a cheesy pick-up line

"How much extra do I have to pay to get you?" I asked, with a grin I hoped was teasingly suggestive.

He blinked, registering what I had said for a moment, and then smiled. "But you're ordering one of the few vegetarian options on our menu. If I was thrown in, you'd have to be a carnivore."

I laughed. "Maybe I am a carnivore. Maybe I just like cheese with my boys."

He gave the first guffaw I had had heard in a long time, one of those deep belly laughs that fill the causer with glee at creating such an exuberant sound. Turning to look around him quickly, he leaned over and whispered, pushing the mike away from his mouth.

"I'm about to get off work. If you wait a minute, I'll share some cheese with you. Can't vouch for the boy part, though."

I winked at him. "The boys aren't for you, they're only for me. You'll have to make do with the cheese."

"I can handle that," he said, grabbing my order from the counter beside him and handing it to me through the window, an icon of professionalism.

As he reached forward to put the soda into my waiting hand, he whispered, "I'll come find you in the parking lot," before leaning back and then, with a tone startlingly loud in comparison, he said, "Thanks for your order, Ma'am. We appreciate your business."

I grinned, gesturing back at him with my soda, before heading to the back of the lot, where I parked my car. I nervously started eating my sandwich as I waited, feeling the grease seep through the paper, conscious that it was getting on my fingers and probably on my face, aware that any "real" girl would not be eating right now, would be applying

135

makeup and preserving a cleanly scented mouth for the awaited boy, but I was too hungry to do that.

He did not seem to have any issues with grease, because he opened up my car door, sliding into my passenger seat with a white paper bag of his own.

"I've got my cheese," he said, grinning, eyeing my half-consumed one. "Was it good?"

I nodded, smiling, lips pushed together, my mouth still full of food (typical). He smiled back and, without taking his eyes off me, opened the bag, unfolded the paper wrapper, and chowed into his sandwich. We sat like that, in silence, the only sound the crinkling of paper and the chewing of our jaws. I wondered what to say. This was definitely an entirely new situation for me, and I had no idea how to proceed.

I mean, who picks up a man at a drive-through window? I did notice, despite my second-guessing, how much more he looked like Ashton Kutcher than I had realized, and how much I really wanted to see him naked, but sadly, it felt like a lot of careful strategizing had to happen to get us there, and I was not sure I was up to it at this late hour.

"Do you usually get your cheese sandwiches this late at night?" he asked, between mouthfuls.

I had finished my sandwich by this point and was neatly folding the wreckage over and over between my hands, hoping the methodical behaviour would appease my nerves.

I nodded. "I don't do the cheese sandwiches very often. I save them for nights when it's too late to get anything else."

"So I guess I should thank my lucky stars Jack in the Box was already closed, eh?"

I grinned back at him, stashing my paper trash in the pocket along the side of the door. The O.C.D. folding had to stop. I was ready for the responsibility of un-busy hands. Looking over at him, I watched him chew his last bite and fold his wreckage into a neat little rectangle. He glanced down at the pocket on his door before thinking twice and looking over at me.

136

"What should I do with—"

Just as I was reaching forward to take it, he shook his head. "Never mind," he said, "give me yours."

Confused, I extracted my rectangle of waste out of the door and handed it over to him.

"Be right back," he called out as he sprinted out of my car, tossing the papers into the trashcan at the end of the parking lot before loping back over.

I smiled at his lanky body and his face, which was even cuter than Ashton Kutcher's. He slipped into his seat and looked at me expectantly.

"Where shall we go?" he asked.

"Where do you want to go?" I had no idea how to take it from here.

"I don't know." He winked at me. "Didn't you pick *me* up?"

I laughed. "Yeah, I guess you're right." Pause. Hesitation. Then I revealed, "I've never done this kind of thing before."

Now it was his turn to laugh. "Oh yeah? Could have fooled me. Everything about you seemed totally natural."

I shook my head. "That's just the act. Believe me. Now that I've got you, I have no idea what to do with you!"

Grinning, he took my right hand and lifted it to his lips for a quick kiss. "Never fear, my lady. I've got an idea or two." He released my hand, letting it rest back on my thigh. "Do you mind driving since we're already here?"

"You got it." Turning the car on, I slid into reverse and manoeuvred to face the street. "Just tell me where to go."

"Wait," he cried out, and I slammed down on the brake.

"What? What?" I thought, for a second, that I might have killed an animal.

His face a little flushed with embarrassment, he said, "Sorry to scare you. I just thought of something."

"Oh. Okay." I turned to look at him, awaiting further instructions.

"Give me a sec."

137

He leapt out of the car and, once again, loped across the parking lot, only this time to what looked like a small black car. He popped open the trunk, rummaged inside for a moment, grabbed something bulky-looking, and then locked everything back up again.

As he got closer to me, I could see that he was carrying a bottle of wine and two Styrofoam cups. Grinning as he approached my open car window, he poked his arms through, showing me his recently remembered booty. I laughed, taking the bottle of wine and the cups so that he could open the car door.

"I totally forgot I had this bottle in my car. I was at a birthday party earlier tonight, and I'd brought the wine, but then they already had so much liquor, my friends insisted I take it back with me. The cups, well, they've been sitting in my car for a while, but I think they're still usable. Styrofoam never disintegrates, right?"

"Don't think so," I replied, smiling at him and the obvious joy of his discovery. There was something adorable about the prospect of drinking trunk-temperature white wine out of Styrofoam cups. "But you still haven't told me where we're going…?"

"Oh. Right. Okay." He paused, contemplating. "Okay. Turn out of the parking lot. Make a right. I'll direct you. We're going to make another right at the next major intersection."

"No problem." Once again, I turned the car on and moved to pull out of the lot. We did not speak much, just him giving me directions and me following them.

We did not drive far, only into Pasadena. He navigated us to the corner of Orange Grove and Colorado Boulevard, before motioning for me to pull into an empty parking space. I still had no idea what his plan was. I probably should have been more cautious and nervous, but, call me naïve, I could not imagine being raped by someone transporting two picnic-ready cups for a bottle of wine that clearly came with good intentions.

138

Looking like a kid at his birthday party, he bounded out of the car, jumped around to the other side to open my door, and then, after collecting both cups and bottle from me, he offered an arm for me take. Like two civilized souls on their way to join a Seurat painting, he escorted me across a grassy lawn, down a short street (it still did not occur to me to feel nervous), and to the entrance of the Colorado Street Bridge, designed and built in 1913 and connecting Pasadena with Eagle Rock. It was one of the most beautiful landmarks in the area.

"Where are we going?" I asked, at last, dying of curiosity.

"Here, of course!" Walking onto the bridge, he escorted me to the first nook, a curved space to the side of the bridge framed by stone bench-like seats.

"Have a seat," he said, gesturing downwards, and I complied.

Once I sat down, he, more like an employee of the Ivy than an employee of In-N-Out, deftly uncorked the wine and poured it gracefully into the two cups. Smiling with a combination of self-consciousness and amusement, I took my cup.

"Cheers," he said, knocking his gently against mine.

"Cheers," I said back, looking at him over the top of the cup as I sipped.

It was a good wine, crisp and dry, and I took another swallow before lowering the cup back down. He was still standing over me at this point, but once I put my cup on the ledge, he came over, standing with his legs on either side of mine. Only one car had driven by us since we had arrived. I had no idea what time it was, but I figured we had a little space before morning rush hour would begin. Even though the sun was starting to rise, the sky was still gray and hazy, and I could clearly see the moon above us. I became aware of the height of his crotch and how close it was to my face.

"Come here," I told him, placing my hands on his thighs and tugging him forward.

139

Smiling at me, he stepped closer, bringing his hips inches away from my mouth.

"Do you mind?" I asked, my fingers reaching for his belt buckle.

"Not at all," he said, giving his head an easy shake from side to side.

I unhooked the buckle, slipping the belt through the loops, so that I could unbutton, and then unzip, his pants. The simple pressure of my hand running the zipper downward was enough to make him moan and arch back slightly. I grinned, slipping my hand between the crevice formed by his now unzipped pants, cupping him gently in my palm. He moaned again. He was hard and curved against my hand, the rigidity barely concealed by the cotton covering of his underwear. Tugging his underwear to the side and letting his pants slip down to his hips, I released him. He sprang out, rock-hard, virtually perpendicular and precisely in line with my lips, which I opened to envelop him.

He groaned as my lips wrapped around him, tucked over my teeth so that I would not hurt him, but giving me enough pressure to run back and forth over his cock, which got even harder and more swollen with every lick of my tongue, the veins forming ridges across the skin. I shoved my other hand inside his pants, feeling his balls against the underwear, the dense heat obvious even through the fabric.

I picked up speed, my right hand rubbing his skin back and forth, my lips and tongue sending warm saliva across the tip of his cock, rapid flicks of the tongue matching the tempo of my other movements, while my left hand slowly rubbed his balls back and forth. I could feel his knees wobble, and I increased my pressure but kept the speed constant, teasing him closer to orgasm.

I had almost all of him in my mouth—and what was not in my mouth was in my hand. His balls felt heavier, and his cock felt harder, and I knew he was so close that I could not understand why he was not coming, until, with a gesture as

140

reluctant as it was emphatic, he pushed me off him.

"I'm sorry," he panted, "it's not you. You're fucking amazing. I just can't come here. I hear the traffic going by, and even if no one can really see what we're doing, they must be able to see enough to guess, and I can't lose the self-consciousness. I'm sorry."

Looking at how swollen his cock was, how engorged, I knew he was sorry. I knew how frustrated he must have been, and I had to confess, I felt a certain thrill. Something about the sight of him straining to fit back into his pants, gently and cautiously pulling up the zipper, made me especially conscious of how wet my underwear was.

"Poor little baby," I murmured, grabbing hold of his now re-closed belt and using it to pull myself up.

We were face-to-face, inches apart, and I realized that we still had not kissed. I had never gone down on a boy before kissing him, and I laughed about this inwardly as he pulled me toward him, shoving his tongue in my mouth with the hunger of sexual frustration. This time it was my turn to get wobbly in the knees, and I wrapped my arms around his waist, pulling myself closer, both to steady myself and also to press my pelvis against his.

Both of us moaning now, we were damp with sweat and desire. My underwear was so wet that I wondered if I had leaked onto my jeans. Most importantly, I wondered if he could feel any leakages. We made out on the bridge like hormonally-charged adolescents, tortured and tantalized by the limitations of our circumstance, until I had a flash of inspiration.

"I've got it," I told him, grabbing his hand and leading him back over the bridge.

"Where are we going?" he asked, fumbling with his other hand in his pants.

"Adjusting yourself?" I asked, laughing.

"Yes," he answered, grimace mixing with grin as he looked at me sideways, doing his best to keep up with me while making the appropriate arrangements in his pants.

141

Still holding his hand, I led him back toward my car.

"Are we going somewhere?"

I shook my head. "Not really."

He looked at me, confused. I did not say anything further. I owned a huge beast of a car, an old Volvo station wagon older than my teenage sister, with tinted windows on all sides. I knew there was some reason why a single girl with limited possessions would acquire such a car, and tonight was an indication of the car's untapped potential.

While he stood there, looking at me quizzically, I unlocked the front door before opening up the passenger doors in order to fold down the backs of the passenger seats.

"Can I help in any way?" he asked, still clearly having no idea what I had in mind.

"Nah, I got it," I said, very much distracted by my preparations.

After getting both the seats flat and clearing off whatever stray objects might have been tossed back there, I turned and gestured for him to step inside.

"You should probably crawl in through here. Then I'll crawl in behind you. I don't think there's any way to get the back door closed from the inside."

Looking at me strangely, he clambered through the doorway and over the folded seats. Once he got back there, I could see the light click on behind his eyes, and the smile spread slowly across his face.

"I got it. I know what you're up to. Excellent plan."

Grinning, I piled in behind him, pulling the door shut. Now we were lying alone together in a little igloo of tinted blackness as early morning commuters passed by, unable to see us or suspect what we might be about to do.

I grabbed his belt buckle, tugging him closer. We were finally horizontal, and I wanted to feel him against me. He was pressed up as close as possible, body to body, his hands groping at my breasts, pinching my nipples with his fingertips, sending pulsations throughout my body. If he had not been able to tell my pants were wet before, he must have

142

been able to tell now.

I shoved my hand between belt buckle and skin, feeling his pubic hair as I squeezed my way down, until hand touched cock, and he moaned, his sticky pre-cum coating my fingers. I wrapped my right hand around his cock, loosening his belt and struggling against metal teeth and awkward angles to get his fly open with my left hand. We may have been horizontal, and we might have been protected by the shield of darkened windows, but that did not mean I had the finesse or coordination to get him undressed.

He clearly felt the same way, as my bra simply got shoved down underneath my breasts as they spilled over the newly lowered neckline, elastic pressure making them even perkier than usual. I was rubbing my hand up and down what part of his cock I could easily grab with an urgency made all the more acute by the teasing sensation of his tongue on my nipples.

"Please," I murmured desperately, tilting my hips toward him, and he got the message.

With a quick gesture, my zipper's metal teeth had also been separated, and now his hand was equally shoved inside my pants. I could not believe the hurried commuters with their neat briefcases did not hear our moans as they passed us by. We were immune. I could feel us steaming up the windows, alone in our den of sin, but no one in the outside world could tell what was happening inside the walls of my navy blue Volvo station wagon, and it felt great. With the thrill of the illicit, I moved my hand rougher and faster, wondering if these circumstances would provide the right combination of forbidden and erotic to get him off, or if he would still be too self-conscious to come in my hands.

I did not have to worry about myself. My orgasm came about a minute after his hand went between my legs, the combination of one hand in my drenched pussy, while his other clenched and pinched my nipples, plus the feeling of his hard cock, the blood pulsing through his veins a direct correlation to the speed of my movement, providing all the

143

stimulus I needed. I did not even need his cock inside me. Just feeling it inside my hand was enough, and I came with a loud moan, vibrations everywhere from knees to fingertips, but I did not let up. I did not stop. I kept rubbing him, and the sight and sound of my orgasm was the last straw for a sexually frustrated boy. With one long cry, he came all over the inside of his pants and the inside of my hand—and not a drop escaped to stain the inside of my 1990 station wagon.

What do you do?

Drive him to your house for round two?
(turn to page 145)
or
Drive him back to his car so you can ditch him?
(turn to page 151)

Round two

We lay in silence for a moment, but since it was a car, it was not the most conducive for post-coital cuddling, and, since it was a car, the logical next activity was driving.

"Can I take you somewhere?" I asked. "Would you like to come back to my place? It's slightly more comfortable..."

He grinned. "More comfortable than *this*?" His arm swept around with a flourish. "This is a pretty posh wagon."

I laughed. "Yes. While that is true, the point remains—would you like a padded mattress? Would you like a change of scene? Or do you wanna stay right here, like this?"

"Do you always micro-manage?" he asked, the grin still on his face. He paused. I was not sure if it was a rhetorical question, but I chose not to answer, regardless. He filled the silence by continuing. "I'd love to go back to your place, if you don't mind."

"I don't mind," I said. "I think that would be grand."

"Fabulous, micro-manage away!" he exclaimed, with a wink and a friendly kiss, so I could not take it personally.

I smiled at him as we gathered our clothes, before changing position back to the front seats of the car. It was a short drive back to my apartment, and we did not talk much along the way. It was an easy silence, though, and his left hand drifted to my right thigh as I drove, my right hand comfortably resting on his left thigh.

I parked the car, and we walked companionably up to my apartment, hand in hand, as though we had known each other significantly longer than an hour or two. I would have marveled at this, but I was not really paying attention. I was too busy trying to figure out what I was going to do with him now that we were back at my place. I realized that my invite had not been entirely well thought-out. This was a guy who had recently served me a cheese sandwich, and now he was

145

sitting in my living room, waiting for me to get him a glass of water. What was that about? What was I supposed to do next?

"What would you like to do?" I asked brightly, as if I had not really thought about it at all.

He looked at me and grinned. "Whatever you want!"

"Whatever *you* want," I tossed back at him.

"Really?" he asked, without missing a beat.

"Uh...I think so!"

There was a pause while I wondered if I should inquire what, exactly, he had in mind, or if I should wait for him to elaborate. I waited.

"You wanna take some photos?"

"Take some *photos*?" I was not sure what he was getting at.

"Yeah. Photos. Pix. Could be fun."

I realized two things immediately. One, that I did not know this boy at all. Second, that I had never done this before, but he was right—it *could* be fun, although I reserved judgment on the latter until I had more information.

"Okay," I said, slowly, feeling a bit hesitant but still ready to play. "How do we start?"

I figured he had obviously done this kind of thing before, or at least given it some thought. I would let him take the reins.

"Really?" he asked, with wonder, as though waiting for me to re-neg on the plan.

"Sure. Tell me what you want me to do."

"Ok..." he said slowly, drawing out the word as if it was a whole sentence. I watched the gears turning in his head. "You want to show me your closet?"

"My closet?" I had assumed clothes would be coming off. I did not expect them to be going *on*.

"Yeah. Undressing is always more fun when you've dressed up."

I bought that. "Okay. Let's go. It's this way."

Standing up, I let him follow me out of the living room

146

and into my bedroom. There were so many things about this evening that stood out as thoroughly bizarre, I had (almost) stopped being surprised by how events were turning out. Still feeling a bit of trepidation, I opened the closet door and stepped to the side. I did not know what he was looking for, but I figured I would let him do that part on his own.

He took a quick overview of everything, rapidly rifling through the shirts, pants, even the dresses, before turning back to me.

"Do you know what you want to wear?" he asked.

"No," I replied, shaking my head. "You go first."

He squinted his eyes a bit as he tried to gauge exactly what was going on in my head. I was not sure what he figured out, because, for some reason, he decided it would be okay to ask if he could wear one of my dresses.

"One of my dresses?" I tried my best not to raise my voice, to keep my cool, not to reveal the amusement that was tugging at my lips.

"Yeah." He grinned nervously. "Is that okay with you?"

"Uh, sure. I guess so. Do you know which one?"

He turned back to the closet. "How about this one?" he asked, pulling out a clingy, stretchy number with blue stripes.

"Really?" I asked, doing my best not to sound like a conservative housewife, as if this kind of thing happened to me all the time.

"Yeah. Why? Ya think it won't fit?"

He looked quizzically at the dress, then down at his body. Right. Size was what was concerning me at this point!

"It should fit. It's pretty elastic. It should just expand around your hips. And you *are* pretty skinny. I bet our sizes aren't that far apart."

He smiled with glee, slipping the dress off the hanger. Holding it up to his body one more time, as though evaluating it for purchase, he then turned away from me, as if suddenly shy. He first tugged his shirt over his head, then his pants and boxers off his legs. I laughed at the shot of his

147

skinny, slightly hairy legs and his white ass, and he turned to look at me over his shoulder. He grinned at me nervously. He was definitely shy. I did not blame him.

"I'm sorry," I said, with a conciliatory tone. "I didn't mean to laugh. I'm sorry. I wasn't laughing at you, just kind of at the situation…"

He just grinned, pulling the dress over his head and over his hips. It was kind of a perfect fit, although his lack of female curves made it look a little strange. Nonetheless, it *did* fit, and it reached all the right places. I reached over to tug it straight, but just after I had pulled the dress halfway down his thighs, he, with a naughty smirk, lifted it back up to hip level, exposing a cock that was semi-hard and on its way to getting stiffer.

I looked up at him, startled and pleased. He smiled at me.

"Wanna take some photos?" he asked.

"Photos? Of you? Now?"

He nodded. I shrugged, more to myself than for him. Why the hell not? There was not anything wrong with what we were doing, certainly nothing that kinky, and I was still young enough that it was good to keep trying new things. Maybe it was a little off the beaten path, but that seemed all the more reason to do it.

All these thoughts ran through my head as I rummaged in my desk drawer to retrieve my digital camera. I checked the battery. We were all good. Turning back around to face him, he was standing with his back against my closet, facing me. I suddenly felt nervous again. I glanced down and almost dropped the camera. The cock that had been sort of hard before was now enormous. It was jutting out beneath the dress, somehow even more aggressively tumescent when seen in contrast with the feminine fabric.

I did not know what to think about the fact that I was really turned on. I kind of wanted to step forward, to touch it, to rub it, to make him harder and even more swollen, but then he started doing that himself. Leaning against the

148

sliding closet door, his right hand began moving back and forth over the tightening skin of his cock, index finger cupped around from the bottom, thumb across the top, kind of tugging on the skin, his eyes never leaving my face.

Feeling completely mesmerized, my eyes darting back and forth between his cock and his face, I slowly brought the camera to my face, and, with only the briefest of glances at the view screen—I wanted to see this for myself, direct, not through a third party electronic device—I started snapping pictures. He knew I was taking them, but he never looked at the camera. His eyes were trained at my face. The only sign that things were changing was through his speed. As I clicked, he picked up his pace, going faster, the look in his eyes becoming more intense, more primal, and more hungry.

The dress did not make him more feminine. It did not make him look gay. If anything, it accentuated his masculinity, drawing attention to the discrepancy between the clingy stripes and the aggression in both his movements and expression. While it would never, in a million years, have occurred to me to suggest this as an activity, certainly not a sexual one, I had to admit to myself that it was hot. I was dripping all over my thighs, I could feel my clitoris swelling, and all without any physical contact whatsoever. I could not take my eyes off him.

Transfixed, I watched him go faster. I watched his eyebrows furrow. I watched his eyes squint slightly. I watched the lines form on his forehead. I watched the intensification occur as if I was not even in the room, until I could not take it anymore. I tossed the camera on my bed and dropped to my knees, putting him into my mouth. I realized, when he moaned, just how silent the two of us had been. I loved hearing his moan, I loved the uncontrollable gasp of pleasure that slipped out of his mouth, and I wanted more.

He was so hard that there was not much I had to do. I knew what had to happen next—the tongue teasing and the hand twisting. I knew when to start and when to stop. I knew

149

how to make him even harder, how to make him beg to let me release him, and I waited until I heard the stammered "Please" emerge between pants and then, with a grin only I knew about, I picked up speed, maintaining constant pressure, counting in my head: one, two, three, four...

I knew that, by the time I got to ten, he would be done, and I was right. When I hit eight, his hands banged on the closet door, and he came like an explosion against the back of my throat.

I slid my hand back and forth a couple more times, slowly, letting the last bit of cum mix with the saliva in my mouth, and then I swallowed. I stayed down on the floor a little longer, licking him clean, before I stood up. He grinned at me, somehow now adorable in the dress, all the aggressive desire gone, and I grinned back.

"Did you like that?" he asked.

"I might have liked it as much as you," I told him.

"I highly doubt that! Now want to help me get this dress off?"

"Nope. That's your job. I'm taking the photos!"

With that, I stepped back, grabbing the camera back off the bed. Documenting the final striptease was something I could not miss!

You win. You got the photos, the memories, and a boy who owes you one.

150

Ditch him

We lay in silence for a moment, but it was a car, so not the most conducive for post-coital cuddling, and, by this time of early morning, I knew I had to go to bed. This had been a very long and very adventurous night, and it was definitely time for a shower and some sleep—alone.

"Can I bring you back to your car?" I asked. "I'm sorry, but I've really got to get some sleep."

I tried to say it as gently as I could, because I did like this guy, but my god, this had been one hell of an evening.

"Yeah, sure, no problem," he said, seemingly not at all offended. "I'm pretty beat, too. Working the late night shift always drains me...Although, I must say you were hot enough to distract me from my fatigue..."

Letting his voice trail off, he slowly ran his finger across my stomach. It sent shivers down my spine, and I wrapped myself around him for one more kiss. But one more kiss was all it was. After some fantastic French kissing acrobatics, I detangled myself and began fixing my clothes. He got the message and did the same.

I climbed out the side passenger door, opening the main wagon door for him. He kissed me one more time, our first public daytime kiss, and then we made our way to our respective car seats. The drive back to the In-N-Out parking lot was almost too brief, since I was not quite ready to let him go, knowing that there was a very good chance that, if previous boy behaviors were any standard by which to judge, I would never see him again, but I also had that gross need-to-brush-my-teeth feeling, and so separation was inevitable and the right thing to do.

When we got to the lot, I pulled up beside his beat-up black Honda Civic, smiling at the KXLU bumpersticker on the rear.

151

"Bye-bye," he said, with one more lingering kiss and a sweet little fondle of my hand.

"Bye," I said, too tired to feel any real sense of loss.

He let the door close gently behind him (you have to love a man who knows not to slam a car door) and stepped toward his car. I had just put my car into reverse when he knocked quickly on the passenger side window. I leaned over to roll it down, looking at him with curiosity.

"I almost forgot to give you this!"

I looked at what "this" was. It was the In-N-Out receipt, with his phone number scribbled on the back. Cute.

"Thanks," I said.

"Call me," he said.

I rolled the window back up and reversed out of the parking lot. It was definitely time to brush my teeth and go to sleep. The decision about whether or not to call him would come later, but I liked the feeling of knowing it was mine to make.

You win. Do not forget to floss.

152

Escape the smarminess

Hot as Natalie was, I was all too aware of her hetero-normative leanings, and the now damp and sort of hairy guy that those leanings included. It was too late, and I was too sexually satiated, to feel motivated to deal with either of them. I hauled myself out of the pool, too lazy even to make my way to the stairs.

"Where are you going?" Natalie drawled, with post-sex bleariness.

Mark's arms and legs were wrapped around her, and he was doing something with his tongue on her neck. The bitchy part of me wanted to spit out that I was surprised she had even noticed, but I had too much Southern politeness engrained in me, so I just murmured something about it being late and needing to get home.

Natalie reached her arm out to me, either as a gesture of goodbye or an attempt to pull me back in, but I had already moved too far for her to reach me, so she just turned back to Mark and his tongue, which had snaked its way over to her mouth.

I left the two of them like that, going to dry off and dress. I stuck both my underwear and bra in my bag, as they hardly seemed worth the effort. This early in the morning, I did not think I would see anyone on the way to my car, and if I did, who cared. There were few things as disconcerting as pulling undergarments on over damp skin.

I did not say goodbye, and they did not seem to notice, as the stairwell door clicked behind me, and I found my way to the elevator. I was so tired that I felt almost numb, and, as I leaned against the mirrored wall of the elevator, I was glad that my drive home would only take ten minutes. I just wanted to feel blissfully horizontal and peacefully alone.

My relatively direct descent to street level was

153

interrupted by a stop on the sixth floor. As the elevator purred to a halt, I glanced half-heartedly into the mirror to make sure I did not look a complete mess. My hair actually was not too bad. I had expected total post-pool frizz, but it seemed to be drying into cooperative ringlets. While my makeup was definitely smudged, it seemed smudged into that post-cocaine party binge fashionista look, so even that was okay. There was not much I could do about the fact that my shirt had gone practically transparent on my damp skin, leaving my nipples as pointy little orbs, but it was no worse than most of Britney Spears's outfits, so I just looked up, ready to say good morning with the right combination of perky confidence and casual disinterest.

The elevator door slid open, and we stared at each other. Of all the people I might have expected to see in a downtown elevator around six in the morning, Dara was not one of them. Although, at the same time, after thinking about it for a second, Dara also seemed to be an appropriate choice. Both of our surprised expressions became huge grins, and she bounded into the elevator to give me a big bear hug, the kind that lifted me off the ground and pressed my slightly damp body against hers.

"Girl, you're wet. What's that about?"

Her arms still tightly wrapped around me, she stretched her head back enough to get a good look at my face.

My arms pinned to my sides, there was not much I could do but answer. "I was in your pool, dumbass."

"In the pool? Now?" She dropped me gently to the floor, lifting up her wrist to examine the time. "You definitely know how to party!" she said, with a big grin, and I became all the more aware of the conspicuous nature of my nipples.

I just smiled back at her, not really wanting to go into any more detail, reluctant to tell her what I had been doing, but also not wanting to tempt her into going back up there and possibly continuing the "party." I did not want her to meet Natalie and Mark, and I certainly did not want to meet

154

them again, myself.

"And where are you headed now, party girl?" she asked, with a flirtatious grin.

"Now I'm finally headed home."

Her face fell. "Oh no. Tell me it's not true."

"Dara. It's super late. Time for little girls to go to bed."

"Does that mean I have to go to bed, too…?" With a wink, she paused for a second, looking again at her watch. "You know, you're right," she continued slowly, as the elevator began to open its doors onto the lobby, "but it still feels like a long way for a sleepy girl to have to drive home, and especially with no food in her stomach. How about you take a quick pit stop off at my place? I'm just on the fourth floor. I'll make you some breakfast, and then you can decide if you want to crash in my king-size bed or make the drive home then?"

I reflected. The "long drive" was only about ten minutes, but I was still tempted. I had found Dara hot from the first time I met her, when she had had me sit on her lap while showing a group of mutual friends some new music videos she had recently worked on. While everyone else was oohing and ahhing, all I could think about was her body directly beneath mine, and the way her hands had stayed around my waist as she helped me stand back up.

She had been dating someone then, so nothing happened, but the tension was so thick, it almost made conversation impossible. I did my best to avoid being alone with her, and I think she did the same, because the two of us knew that physical contact would be inevitable.

There was one night, though, late, when I had had to get my coat from her apartment when all our other friends were down the hall. She had walked me there, and then had come in with me while I rummaged around for my things, and there was this moment, when I stood up, and she stood next to me, and a carnal desire took over my entire body, and we both stepped forward toward each other, but then Bridget came bounding in to get *her* coat—and the moment was over.

Then Dara was travelling for a bit, and then I was dating the guy who was now my latest ex, and we had not seen each other for a while, even though I had heard she was single again, and now—the offer. I was tired, and I knew I smelled of chlorine, but I also knew that if I went home, I would only lie in bed thinking of what I walked away from. Should I stay to find out if I had a chance with Dara? Or should I do the smart thing and save myself for a time when I was a little more awake, and it was a little less late?

What do you do?

Take yourself home to enjoy the pleasure of your own company?
(turn to page 157)
Take the elevator back upstairs with the unexpected lesbian?
(turn to page 162)

Take yourself home

I leaned over and gave Dara a goodnight kiss—on the lips—slightly longer than platonic but not complicated enough to get messy. She responded with a hunger I had to think twice about to tear myself away from.

"I'd love to test out your king-size bed," I told her, "but I'd prefer to do it when I have other things on my mind than falling asleep. Rain check, please?"

She grinned. "That sounds like a great idea," she replied, leaning over to give me one more kiss on the lips. "Will you call me when you're rested?"

I nodded. "Sure."

"Like in a few hours?"

I laughed. "Absolutely."

At least her interest was clear, even if my vision was starting to get hazy. Time to get myself home before morning rush hour traffic kicked in, or I would be sure to pass out at the first bottleneck. With one last awkward smile, I sprinted out of the elevator, doors closing neatly beside me, whisking a hot lesbian upstairs to an empty king-size bed, and leaving me to make my way through an otherwise empty lobby.

The suits were starting to fill the sidewalks, and SUVs the streets, as I pulled out of my parking space and onto Broadway. Even though it was pretty bright outside, it was early enough that I made it home without any excessive traffic. It could not have been more than ten or fifteen minutes before I had parked my car in my usual space.

I staggered up the stairs, squinting into L.A.'s unrelenting Eastside sun. I thought briefly of turning back to my car to grab the extra sunglasses from the glove compartment, but it was not worth it. I made my way to my apartment, half blind, and gratefully stepped into the dark

157

living room. All the blinds were closed, thank God, and I instantly felt more alive, as well as relieved that the first time Dara might make out with me would not be when I reeked of chlorine.

Unfortunately, I was too tired to spare myself, or my bedclothes, so I fell into bed still sticky from the chlorine. It was a mistake I regretted almost immediately. There was just enough of a smell to make my insomnia kick in, so I hauled my half-asleep ass into the shower. Leaning against the tiled wall was all I could do as the water drummed over my head and shoulders, rivulets racing across my chest and stomach, hips and legs. My eyes closed, I felt almost sedated by exhaustion.

I tried to run through all the events of my evening, everything that had happened since I last left the house, but it felt too chaotic for my sleep-deprived brain. Giving up on any kind of mental catalogue, I just let the water make its soothing process over my skin. It did not take long for my brain to dictate its own course, and I shut the water off, hurrying into bed, to complete the narrative.

I was half damp, but that did not matter. At least I did not smell like chlorine. Eyes closed, head silent, I let my mind wander as it wanted, my fingers drifting downwards, between my legs.

He was still on the massage table, and he was still naked, except for the inadequate excuse for a sheet. I was wearing the French maid outfit, and my breasts were still shoved up to perfection. My feet were encased in ultra-fierce, ultra-pointed high heels, making my legs look like they belonged to an Amazonian supermodel.

I had already teased him to a point of rock-hard frustration, his cock as slippery with lotion as the rest of his carefully massaged skin. I had slid my hand beneath his balls to stroke the crevice of his ass, and he had already oozed cum over my right hand. Now it was my turn, only he did not know it yet.

He was lying on the massage table, viscous white liquid

158

in neat droplets across his stomach and between his thighs. I turned around to the small sink in the corner, washing my hands and dampening a small towel. Whisking the towel over his skin, I cleaned him off, and it was only after I had rinsed the towel off in the sink that he opened his eyes to look at me.

"Tell me," he began.

"Yes?"

I stepped closer to the table. He reached out with his hand toward my skirt. I stepped closer. With the one finger that was most outstretched, he tried to flick the fabric upwards.

"Are you wearing anything under that?"

Not moving closer or farther away, just standing still as if my stiletto heels were screwed into the floor, about an inch or two away from his most extended finger, I answered with the smallest of head shakes.

He strained a little bit farther. I did not move. His finger did not reach more than the outmost edges of lace. He strained some more. This time he got close enough to graze the bottom of the skirt, but not enough to get proper momentum. My skirt stayed where it was, as did my feet, at least, until I bent over.

With a control that would make any stripper proud, I bent over, slowly, slowly, slowly, my body pivoting so that my ass was pointed toward his face. I was too far away for him to reach, but that did not mean he did not try. He tried to touch the bare skin of my smooth white ass, he tried to run his fingers along my curves, but all he managed to do was trace them in the surrounding air.

Satisfied that he had gotten enough of a look to make him want more, I slowly straightened, spinning around to face him like a ballerina in a music box. Even though he was still damp from having his latest cum cleaned off, his eyes looked at me with puppy dog hunger. He did want more. I smiled.

"Would you like to touch?" I asked, mockingly.

159

His only response was to reach forward again, fingers angling not for ass this time, but for anything they could access, which was still nothing. I took pity on him (and on myself) and stepped forward. He grabbed my thigh and pulled me to him.

"Can you lower this table?" he asked, addressing my thigh.

"Of course. How low do you want it?"

"Can you bring it down about a foot?"

I nodded, grabbing hold of the handle and winding it counterclockwise, dentist chair style. With a well-oiled hum, the table receded, several inches at a time, until he was at the desired height.

"Okay, now what?"

Without saying anything, he took hold of my other thigh with his other hand and positioned me so that I stood squarely above his face. I felt surprised that I had never thought of using the table this way before. With the greed of the starved, he began to eat me out. First with slow, sensual licks, then with a more aggressive lapping, he circled and stroked. He swallowed, and I dripped, his movements getting faster, unrelenting, leaving me standing there, weak-kneed and consumed with desire. I did not usually come from tongue alone, but in this case, it was all about first times. He licked and sucked, my clitoris between his lips, every part of my pussy wet and swollen and aching for more contact.

When I looked down, all I saw was the perfect extended circumference of my French maid skirt, but I felt his breath and his mouth and his tongue, the prodding and licking and kissing and sucking intensifying, both of us growing hotter and more swollen, his extended cock the most obvious part of his body in my line of vision.

I came all over his face, dripping and knees buckling, hands clenching table, his hands wrapped around my thighs, and I moaned with the sweet release, with the waves of vibrating pleasure, and all I could see was my skirt and the engorged veins of his cock, and I could not think of anything

160

else I would rather look at.

With the utmost satisfaction that accompanies an orgasm well-earned and a sleep long overdue, I rolled over, pulling the blanket over my body, and closed my eyes again, this time for a deep sleep. I knew it would come easy. There was no desire left in my body to keep me awake—for now. Tomorrow I would call Dara.

You win. Sleep well—you need the rest.

The unexpected lesbian

She grinned, pressing the number four button quicker than I had ever seen her move, and we made our way back up the building. We did not say much on the way, just looked at each other. It had been a while since I had seen her, but she still looked the same. Her hair was in its usual tousled state, shaved on the sides, with a strip down the middle that was probably two or three inches long, eyes rimmed with black eyeliner that had clearly been applied hours, if not days, before.

I noticed there were a couple new tattoos, something in Latin across her back, a bird that looked almost like a crane across her right shoulder blade, interwoven with flowers. She looked like Lori Petty in *Tank Girl* meets the Girl with the Dragon Tattoo. In other words, guerrilla hot. She could manage riding a jeep across desert wasteland as easily as wearing sexy lingerie. Obviously, I would rather have seen her taking off the latter than accompany her through the former, but I would have willingly joined either activity, happy to lick the sweat off her dirty, wet skin.

I tried to smile demurely at her as we disembarked from the elevator, and she gave me one of her joyful grins as she bounded after me, before giving me another one of her wrap-around-and-lift-me-up hugs, only this time I was even more aware of the fact that we were alone together, and there was no one hovering on the horizon who could interfere. It felt like being alone with a perfect banana fudge sundae and knowing that no one would watch you eat it—or force you to share. I wanted to eat her ice cream, her banana, and her cherry.

We giggled our way down the hall, mindful of the fact that most people were asleep to the extent that we tried to keep the volume down, but also under the influence of

162

enough late-night delirium to be unable to control ourselves fully. Luckily, we were moving quickly enough that, even if we woke people up, we were gone before they could figure out what was going on, or, worse yet, poke their heads out of their doors to see what was happening.

As we walked, hips brushed against hips, falling into each other as though we were drunk, but we were just tired and giddy. It felt liberating to be so relaxed with her.

She unlocked the door to her apartment and swung it open, waiting for me to step inside before following, then she, too, stepped inside, and the door clicked shut behind us. I turned around to look at her. She just stared at me. Then, as though we had done it a million times before, she spun me around so my back was against the door, and she shoved her tongue down my throat, her aggressive desire echoing the feelings I had struggled with every time I had been around her.

We kissed like that—against the door—like new lovers separated for days, with a hunger made more acute by the familiarity of our bodies, and then, after one last deep, penetrating push into my mouth, she leaned back, grabbed my hand, and pulled me after her further into the apartment.

"Food!" she called out. "What can I make you?"

I traipsed after her, feeling somehow awkwardly juvenile. I could not remember the last time anyone had cooked for me and certainly not breakfast. My ex did not really cook, and beyond that, maybe there were one or two dinners awkwardly prepared by permanent bachelor types. There was something charming about being fixed breakfast, especially after not having slept all night, and I felt flattered even though I knew it probably meant more to me than to her.

"What are your breakfast options?" I asked, perching myself on the edge of the granite kitchen counter.

She came to stand between my legs, manually wrapping them around her waist so that my crotch was pressed at her chest, and my chest was exactly at the level of her mouth.

163

Staring at me thoughtfully, as if the answer was written on my face, she slowly went through her list.

"Hmm…I can make you waffles, or eggs, or boring cereal. I've got some veggie sausage, and French toast is always an option." She reflected further. "That might be it. Have I covered the basics?"

I grinned at her. "That's quite a lot of options. I'm not sure which I'd go for. Maybe eggs?"

"Just eggs?" She seemed a little disappointed.

"You want more complex?"

"Yeah. Bring it on."

I almost laughed at her tough guy stance. Definitely a lot of Lori Petty going on in this kitchen.

"Okay." I paused for a moment. "How about eggs, toast, veggie sausage…and you make it all with your shirt off?"

A slow smile spread across her face. "I can do that."

With the controlled ease of a practiced striptease model, she bent her arms around herself, grabbed hold of the cotton t-shirt, and, with deliberate precision, pulled it over her head. This was all done without my legs leaving her waist, so once her shirt was off, she was still encircled by my knees and calves and thighs, and her now exposed chest was inches away from mine.

It had been a bold move on my part, but I had no idea what I should do next. Her breasts were there, just in front of me, perfectly smooth and rounded, totally soft, the hard nipples a dark shade of pink. I wanted to bite them. She had the most amazing breasts you could ever imagine.

She looked back at me, and then she opened her mouth.

"Now it's your turn to make it even," she said.

I laughed. "No problem."

Feeling clumsier than she had looked doing the same thing, I grabbed hold of my shirt with my hands and, conscious of the fact that now both of us would be both bra-less and top-less, tugged it over my head. She took it from my hand and tossed it on top of hers, over the back of a

164

nearby chair. She made no attempt not to stare.

"Girl, you're hot," she said, a mixture of pleased surprise and satisfaction. "Do you mind?"

I shook my head, not sure what she was asking, but it did not matter, because she was not waiting for a reaction, much less looking at anything above my breasts. Leaning forward, she ran her tongue gently and lightly, around first the right nipple, then around the left. The light trail of her saliva following the tender touch of her tongue made me grip the granite counter with both hands. I shivered slightly, feeling suddenly cold and very much almost naked.

She looked up at me, her index finger tracing its way from my neck, between my breasts, across my stomach, to the button at the top of my jeans—and there it stayed, fidgeting slightly, while her eyes never left mine.

"Feeling shy?"

It was a question, but, like the last one, she did not wait for an answer. While I stared back at her, silent, wishing it was more common for kitchens to have mood lighting, she tugged the button open and peered inside. With a grin upwards, back to face level, she said, with even more pleasure, "Commando style, eh?" before unzipping me to check out the style of pubic hair I was sporting. With a gesture of almost reverence, she ran her fingers across the surface of the hair.

"Do you always run around bra-less and panty-less?" she asked me, a hint of respect in her voice.

Part of me wanted to issue a blasé "yes" in response, but I just stammered something about them being wet and in my bag. Not that it would have mattered, she seemed more interested in the dampness coming out of my pussy than the words coming out of my mouth. I was swollen and dripping, but I felt frozen. I could not move. I could not talk. I just kept staring at her and her gorgeous tits. Even when she was bending over, I could not get them out of my mind.

I reached for her arms, trying to pull her up. I wanted to kiss her, but she would have none of it. She yanked my pants first down to my hips, and then, with a furtive grin, past my thighs and to the floor. Her head took no time at all to get between my thighs, and her tongue was suddenly on my clit with her fingers inside me. I moaned.

I tried to grab her, but her waist was out of my reach, and with my fingers tugging her hair, I felt strangely ineffectual.

"Please," I begged, "I wanna touch you."

At that, she finally stood up, smile on her face, my wetness glistening on her lips.

"No problem."

And then, with the quickest of gestures, her pants, too, were on the clean kitchen floor.

I jumped off the counter, standing naked in front of her equally naked body. I reached forward to hug her, but she stopped me.

"Wait a second," she told me, "I'll be right back."

I stood in the kitchen, staring at the bare modernist cupboards and metal-looking fridge, until she returned. She was wearing nothing but a black strap-on in a black leather harness. I could not help but gasp (the severity of the lighting made it all the more extreme). She laughed at me but not enough to lose momentum. Positioning me so that I was against the counter, her legs on either side of mine, my hands cautiously slid up her thighs, circling the base of this strange cold plastic thing.

"Oh. I forgot."

Without moving, she opened the drawer to my right, reaching in to extract a tube of Target brand lubricant. Now it was my turn to laugh.

"You keep it in the kitchen?" I asked.

She smiled at me. "I'm a Girl Scout."

Squirting a glob onto the end of her plastic cock, she started to rub it across the surface.

"Wait, let me," I told her.

Looking directly into her eyes, I reached forward, wrapping my fingers around the cock, and began to give it a

166

slow hand job, spreading the shiny lubricant all over it. Even though I knew it was plastic, and she knew it was plastic, and it was not really attached to anyone with anything but a leather harness, it did not feel that way. As I ran my fingers back and forth, I could see her eyes glaze over, and I could feel myself ache for her.

I could not help myself. Getting down on my knees, I slipped my tongue over the tip of her cock, sliding the whole thing into my mouth. I was sure it must have tasted of plastic and slime and glycerine, but it felt like her, and, to me, it tasted like her. This time, it was her turn to moan and to grip the counter with her hands. I moved my mouth back and forth over the shaft, reaching between her legs with my right hand as if to grip the base, but, instead, I felt her very wet, very swollen insides, and with my passing touch, I felt a shudder go through her, and I took that as encouragement to press my fingers deeper inside her.

"No," she panted. "I want to fuck *you*."

Pushing me off her as I stood back up, Dara leaned into me, gently pushing her cock into my very wet pussy, pressing me against the dishwasher, the pressure of her hips pushing herself deeper into me, the pressure of her pelvis sending waves of sensation through my clitoris. Somehow, she had reached the perfect angle with no effort whatsoever.

I wrapped my arms around her, pressing her closer to me, her breasts shoved against mine, her cock deep inside me, her ass under my hands, my fingers surely drawing red indentations across her smooth white skin. Finally, she kissed me again, temporarily slowing the pace of her thrusting to shove her tongue hungrily inside my mouth, her lips all over my face, my skin growing damp with her touch and the heat of the room.

She leaned back slightly, giving herself enough room to start making circles across my clitoris, continuing to fuck me with her strap-on, but slower now, more careful, more controlled, each time hovering around the edges of my cunt for a tantalizing split second before shoving her way back in.

167

If I thought I was dying before, now I was really gone.

It took everything I had just to hold on to her, to keep my fingers intertwined in her harness, while I felt myself swelling more and more, the teasing glimpses of orgasm growing closer and closer, the pleasure accelerating, while her speed remained consistently slow and even, until, with a shudder and scream, I grabbed her to me, and she bucked rapidly, the plastic cock feeling as good as any real cock, if not better, the waves of orgasm vibrating my toes, my knees shaking, my entire body consumed with a pleasure she had controlled but which was now running rampant everywhere.

As things swirled back into place, I realized that my eyes were still closed and my knuckles turning white against the countertop. I gently opened both, turning to look at her. She was looking back at me, a grin on her face, sweat across her cheeks.

"That was amazing," I purred in her ear.

"Yes. It was," she murmured back, pressing herself close to me with the upper part of her body while sliding the cock and the attached lower body away.

I pushed her against the opposite counter as I slid down to my knees. I unfastened the harness and eased it down her legs. Slipping it off one ankle, then the next, I pushed my face between her legs, my tongue against her sleek and slippery pussy, paying special attention to the protruding curves of her clitoris. I caressed it with miniature circles, the upward thrust of her hips toward me all the encouragement I needed. I pressed my index finger inside the entrance to her pussy, at enough of a hook that I could feel its tip against the fleshiness of her body's insides, and I was grateful I was a nail-biter.

Waiting to be told no, I tenderly slipped in another finger, then one more, until I had three inside her, all curved forward against her fleshiness, all going in and out with rhythmic precision, my thumb making circles around her even more swollen clit. She offered no resistance.

It was obvious from the start that she did not have far to

168

go, and the combination of three fingers within, and one without, made her moan and gasp, and my only thought was getting her *there*. I forgot about my knees and my fatigue and the unforgiving brilliance of the kitchen lighting. I was too close to see much of anything, anyway. All that mattered was what I felt, and what I felt was heat and wetness and clenching and moaning, her hands gripping my hair when they were not gripping the counter, and the electricity got so intense, I felt like I had my fingers in a socket.

She must have felt like I was running my own fuse box, because I had never heard someone moan so much, or quiver so much, and when she finally came, with a shuddering climax, I thought she might rip my hair out of my head. She was dripping so much over my fingers that I briefly thought I might short-circuit. I licked her clean before standing up to kiss her.

"Now that was really amazing," she panted gratefully, her hands kneading into my lower back to pull me even closer.

I just smiled at her, pleased and satisfied that I had managed to impress the professional lesbian, still in shock that I finally got to have Dara all over my fingers.

You win. Just take a nap before round two.

169

Stick around

I hated his body hair and the gold chain that glistened against it. I felt an adverse reaction to his testosterone, but, as though she could read my mind, Natalie wrapped her body around me from behind, legs at my waist, arms over my shoulders, and whispered in my ear.

"Let's go down to his apartment and put in a movie or something. We'll let him pass out with a beer. He never lasts once a movie starts."

Turning my head to face her, I smiled conspiratorially. "Sounds like a plan. Let's do it."

"What's going on, ladies?" Mark called over his shoulder, swimming in circles around the deep end of the pool.

"Come on, let's go back to your place," Natalie said back to him, climbing up the ladder out of the pool.

I knew I was smitten when even that simple gesture reminded me both of Denise Richards in *Wild Things* or Esther Williams in anything.

Swimming after her, I got to the ladder before Mark, but not soon enough to climb out before he had made it to the ladder himself, placing himself in prime ass-fondling position. He gave me a little squeeze, accompanied by an approving "uh-*huh*," and any affection which I might have had left for him evaporated.

Even though Mark was blissfully oblivious to my growing animosity, Natalie seemed aware enough of what was going on to flash me a sympathetic smile as she handed me a towel.

"We'll get rid of him, don't worry," she whispered to me before turning to hand a towel to her boyfriend.

He swept her up in his arms, giving her first a lingering kiss on her neck before making his way up her throat to her open lips. I grimaced, but luckily no one noticed. What a bizarre relationship. I was still trying to figure out why she stuck with him, why she managed to exude so much pleasantness for someone who was clearly such a tool.

I found out soon enough.

When we got back to his apartment, events unfolded as she had promised. We each took quick rinse-off showers (separately) and collected on the couch in baggy t-shirts and boxer shorts, obviously on loan from Mark. I tried not to think about that fact too much, just grateful that I was out of my wet clothes and not reeking of chlorine anymore.

"Want a beer?" she asked him, and I guessed that beer was an integral part of the plan.

It did not take long until he was sound asleep on the right end of the couch, opening credits of the movie barely over.

She turned to face me, beaming. "All right! Daddy's sleeping, little girls can play…"

I grinned at her. She slid off the couch, sitting on her knees between my legs. Sending a smirk in my direction, Natalie tugged at my shorts until they were down at my ankles. I was not wearing any underwear, since who wears underwear under boxer shorts? She slipped her finger between my pussy lips, sliding it up and into her lips.

"Yum!" she exclaimed, with a grin. "You're tasty!"

I laughed at her. She leaped to her feet. "Wait. Time to really get this party going…"

With a glance over at Mark to make sure he was still sound asleep, she tiptoed over to a file cabinet beside his computer. Slowly and carefully, so as not to make a sound, she pulled the top drawer open. From where I was sitting, I could not tell what was inside. I heard her rummaging around, and then she turned around, triumphant, a small plastic bag in her hands.

"What's that?" I asked quietly, unable to see in the dim light.

"Yummy stuff!" she whispered back, tiptoeing with

171

exaggerated movements back toward me. "As much cocaine as your little nosey could desire."

She shook the bag in front of my nose for added emphasis. I got the point, and this was where I drew the line. Mark might have been bad enough, but this was past my limit. I was too old for this kind of hedonism.

I shook my head as I told her I did not do drugs.

Her face fell. "You don't?"

I shook my head again.

"Oh. Okay. Well, we don't have to do any."

Putting the bag reverently on the coffee table, she turned back to face me. She made a forced grin, with a little too much tooth, and shrugged her shoulders.

"You really don't want any?" she asked again. "Mark's got a cabinet full. It's what he does between movies."

"What he 'does'?" I asked, unclear if he did or dealt.

"Oh, right. Sorry. *Deals*." She laughed. "But does also." She blinked at me. "You don't do it at all?"

I shook my head for what felt like the hundredth time.

"I thought everyone in L.A. did it."

I did not know what to say to that. All I knew was that the moment was long over, if it had ever really been there in the first place, what with Mark snoring against the right end of the couch, little bits of drool sticking out from between his lips.

Standing up, I faced her, giving her an attempt at a goodbye hug. She hugged me back, sort of limply, and I said that I should probably be going.

"It's a bit late for me to stay up without that stuff," I said, an attempt at a joke.

She smiled nervously, clearly not catching the humor. "You can have some if you want…?"

"Nah, that's really okay." There was an awkward pause while both of us searched for what to say next. "Oh. I should change out of this stuff before I go."

"Don't worry about it. Mark will never notice the loss of a pair of boxers, or one of his millions of t-shirts. Take

172

'em."

"Okay." I nodded. "Thanks."

Grabbing my stuff, I gave her one more hug before making my way out of the apartment. I could not remember if I had ever managed to get her phone number, but, by this point, I figured it did not really matter. I just wanted to get home to get some sleep. It had been a long night.

You lose. Better luck next time.

Dahlia Schweitzer is a writer, teacher, and performer currently residing in Los Angeles.

The author of both erotic novels (LOVERGIRL, QUEEN OF HEARTS, I'VE BEEN A NAUGHTY GIRL) and cultural criticism (for outlets including HYPERALLERGIC and THE JOURNAL OF POPULAR CULTURE), Schweitzer's first academic publication, ANOTHER KIND OF MONSTER: CINDY SHERMAN'S OFFICE KILLER is published by INTELLECT PRESS via THE UNIVERSITY OF CHICAGO PRESS.

In addition to her writing, Schweitzer's critically acclaimed, recently re-released album, PLASTIQUE, consists of sexy dance music and spoken-word interludes, designed to enhance the experience of reading her books.

For more information—and to discover the story behind the story of BREATHE WITH ME—please visit...

www.thisisdahlia.com

175